W9-DJA-935

Praise for Pilar Quintana

"Pilar Quintana uncovers wounds we didn't know we had, shows us their beauty, and then throws a handful of salt into them."

YURI HERRERA, author of *Signs Preceding the End of the World*

"How can I sum up everything that fascinates me about Pilar Quintana. Her incredible lyricism. Her path against the unexpected. The tension—razor-sharp, poetic and uncompromising."

SARA MESA

"Pilar Quintana is pure literature."

LARA MORENO

"Quintana has an impressive ability to tell truly deep stories that outwardly appear quite simple. Precise and concrete, her characters so human it's impossible not to empathize with them."

SARA JARAMILLO KLINKERT

•

Praise for Abyss

"What are the abysses that a girl, stunned by the mysteries of her family and the world, peers into? Her apartment is a jungle, her home a supermarket, her country a fog-enclosed mountain range obscuring the cliffs. Readers too fall, stunned, into Pilar Quintana's abyss."

HÉCTOR ABAD

"Pilar Quintana has created a powerful story that contrasts with the hopeless and doomed atmosphere that surrounds the protagonist. In subtle and brilliant prose, in which nature connects us with the symbolic possibilities of literature, the abysses are both real and intimate."

JURY, Alfaguara Novel Prize 2021

"In a powerful, unsettling voice, Pilar Quintana explores the fears of childhood alongside the fragility and violence of adults. With lucidity, innocence, suspense and the labyrinths of desire, she draws an unforgettable map of the heartrending road to freedom."

IRENE VALLEJO

"A voice of strength, one that takes us to the world of a young girl confronting adult reality from a visionary childhood, a truly important voice that resides in each of us and makes this novel so moving. *Abyss* is Pilar Quintana's triple jump."

ANA MERINO

"A work built around small details that can define an entire continent."

Vogue

"Literature must tend to speak of the universal, of the human. *Abyss* speaks of issues that can challenge any reader anywhere in the world. In Quintana's dialogues you can hear the unsaid."

XAVIER VIDAL, Nollegiu Bookstore

"Pilar Quintana is an author of answers. Her work, real, photographic, complex and personal, opens literary windows that have never been written."
MICHAEL WIN

"A novel about women condemned to unfulfilled lives that avoids oversimplification through the opacity of its protagonist and the lovable, almost naive tone, which nonetheless fills the narrator's gaze with pain."
Babelia

"In *Abyss*, something is on the verge of snapping, a rope being pulled by social impositions at one end and the protagonists' true desires at the other, dangerous as a jungle."
InfoLibre

•

Praise for The Bitch

"A very sensual book that gets under your skin. An overwhelming exploration of maternal desire in the beautiful landscapes of Colombia."
LEÏLA SLIMANI

"A searing psychological portrait of a troubled woman contending with her instinct to nurture is at the heart of Colombian writer Quintana's slim, potent English-language debut. The brutal scenes unfold quickly, with lean, stinging prose. Quintana's vivid novel about love, betrayal, and abandonment hits hard."
Publishers Weekly, starred review

"The magic of this sparse novel is its ability to talk about many things, all of them important, while seemingly talking about something else entirely. What are those things? Violence, loneliness, resilience, cruelty. Quintana works wonders with her disillusioned, no-nonsense, powerful prose."
JUAN GABRIEL VÁSQUEZ

"As Damaris's and Chirli's lives take increasingly tragic turns, their restless natures feel increasingly broadly symbolic of the difficulty of domesticating ourselves and others, even when it serves our best interests. An intense story despite its brevity. A somber and sensitive dog-and-owner tale scrubbed clean of the genre's usual sweetness."
Kirkus Reviews

"Tough and beautiful. The language Quintana uses is concise, sober, almost laconic—it is a ruthless language."
HÉCTOR ABAD

"This acclaimed novella follows a woman raising a dog in an isolated community on the Pacific coast. Quintana's depiction of the jungle is unforgettable, with its countless storms, insects and garbage washed up on the beach. This is a powerful, jolting tale about class, motherhood and rage."
The Guardian

"*The Bitch* distills entire social, ethical, and cultural universes into a potent short novel, thanks to Pilar Quintana's remarkable eye for detail and Lisa Dillman's spare yet stirring translation. Set in a coastal town in Colombia, this novel is populated by complex characters outlined with minimalist strokes of absolute precision, and offers a startling, profound portrait of frustrated desire that will stay with the reader for a long time to come."

JURY, National Book Awards (USA)

"Quintana recreates a wild narrative universe in which the voracity of the jungle, the rain, the sea, and the humidity frame the daily life of the characters of this short novel. *The Bitch* is one of the most important contemporary novels in Colombia as it broadens the places, voices, and subjectivities from which everyday life, femininity, and motherhood are depicted and narrated."

Latin American Literature Today

"Simply perfect."

MARGARITA GARCÍA ROBAYO, author of *Fish Soup*

"A vivid, powerful book, with a tragic core."

Sunday Times

"Engrossing. *The Bitch* is a subtle, moving novel about a struggle to overcome loneliness in an eerie place, among memorable people and animals."

Foreword Reviews

"Set on Colombia's Pacific coast, *The Bitch* is a novel that holds the controlled and natural perfection in the narration until the very end."

World Translations Review

"Pilar Quintana's novella manages to tackle, with the lightest of touches, a striking range of profound themes, from poverty and class inequality to loneliness, loss and repentance. ... This is a wonderfully nuanced meditation on family ties and society's demands, and the central relationship between Damaris and Rogelio is both touchingly tender and grittily believable."
New Internationalist

"*The Bitch* by Colombian writer Pilar Quintana is a devastating portrayal of the aching, unbearable weight that can be felt from guilt, violence, the drive to nurture and the need for human connection."
Shelf Awareness

"*The Bitch* is as exacting, unsettling and somber as the jungle where it's set, as contained as the sky in the book, ready to burst."
MELBA ESCOBAR, *El País*

"*The Bitch* takes hold and won't let go, like the snout of a ferocious animal. Even when recounting intense, profound violence, it does so with a beauty that transports readers to a jungle in which nature reminds us that deep down, we're all just animals trying to survive solitude and sadness."
MAYRA SANTOS-FEBRES, *El País*

"*The Bitch* does not leave us entirely unscathed. Literature—the *mot juste*, creative and true—can transport us to depths difficult to forget. That is the case here."
LUIS ALONSO GIRGADO, *Diario de Arousa*

"This book changes you. It looks deeply into mother-hood, cruelty, and just how unyielding nature can be, with its wild Colombian coastal landscape, which is as gorgeous as it is brutal. The result is unforgettable."
MARIANA ENRÍQUEZ

"Like the themes it explores, Quintana's prose is stark and somewhat grim. Quintana's book is an engrossing, engaging read that can be enjoyed over a few hours, and one of the best examples of *Wendepunkt*—an unexpected turn of events—I have come across in a very long time."
Harvard Review Online

"Sardonic and pitch-black, *The Bitch* begins when childless Damaris brings an orphaned puppy home to the shack she shares with her fisherman husband—what ensues is written with such viciousness that it slices all the way down to the bone."
Vox

"*The Bitch* stands out for the great economy and literary quality of the prose and its ability to display extraordinary oppression amid great openness and geographic immensity. You can read this book without stopping—its story is told in a way that is serene, firm, and luminous."
ALONSO CUETO, Jury for the Premio Biblioteca de Narrativa Colombiana

"A perfect novel in its apparent simplicity. A story to be read in one go, in which everything converges in a masterfully described small drama. It seems to be written without effort and flows naturally, leaving behind traces deep and precise, luminous and tremendous."

ANA RODA FORNAGUERA, former Director of Colombia's National Library

"Beautifully captures the eerie, wild setting near both the jungle and the ocean. The characters are unforget-table—a gorgeous heartbreak of a novel."
BookRiot

"This is a book suffused with privation, in which the jungle is made everyday rather than exoticized, and it's exponentially more powerful for that. Each of its 155 pages—and its unflinching ending—are focused on showing us how Damaris's life is inexorably stripped down to its bare nerves; language isn't in service of aesthetics here, but of a surgically precise excavation of a life at a point of extremis."
Bookmunch

"A searing psychological portrait of a troubled woman contending with her instinct to nurture is at the heart of Colombian writer Quintana's slim, potent English-language debut—Quintana's vivid novel about love, betrayal, and abandonment hits hard."
Booklist

"Pilar Quintana weaves human nature and the chaos of the universe together with extraordinary mastery. This is a novel full of mysteries about unfulfilled desire, guilt, and the places where love still exists."
GABRIELA ALEMÁN, author of *Poso Wells*

"I loved this powerful parable about rage and disempowerment. There's a vitally important message contained here about compassion and transformation, what it means to be a caretaker for the vulnerable and needy, and who gets acknowledged for their labour in society versus who gets ignored. The class differences are subtly but powerfully captured, and the jungle setting effectively evokes a sticky, sweaty heat. An important story for our times."
JULIANNE PACHICO, author of *The Anthill*

"A raw yet beautiful story about maternity and the jungle."
HAY FESTIVAL

"Pilar Quintana has created a psychological tale that sweeps and drags us like the waves of the sea."
El Tiempo

"To narrate the baroque jungle and American sea with such sobriety is a great triumph."
Semana

"*The Bitch* is far from simple in its brevity, communicating an inner universe that readers can easily identify with, by having experienced similar circumstances, reliving childhood, or relating to the portrayal of the landscape and those who inhabit it. This novel is a little gem that reminds me, in its intensity and fluidity, of *The Old Man and the Sea* by Hemingway, or *The Pearl* by Steinbeck."
El Nuevo Día

"A profound and moving drama about life and destiny."
WMagazín

"A tale narrated with skill and a steady hand."
El Espectador

"*The Bitch* is a chronicle of brutal oppression against women. This novel is chilling, simple, brief, raw—a real literary event."
La Vanguardia

"A powerful text about a woman in revolt who doesn't fully give in to suffering. This short yet intense novel's tour de force is its painting of a sordid violence about to explode at any second."
Le Monde

"In three words: singular, stifling, disquieting."
Lire

"Like Rachel Cusk, Pilar Quintana writes beyond the story. These pages flicker with hope and recurrent violence, shadows cast on and by her protagonist Damaris as she rescues a pup whose fecund, wild nature unearths primordial longing and resentments. Polished down to the line."
KRISTEN MILLARES

"A fierce exploration of maternal desire and of unconditional love, *The Bitch* is a cruel, unforgettable, and deeply intelligent story. A big and beautiful discovery."
Page des Libraires

"An extremely sad story that sinks the reader into the main character's emotional void. With an unsparing and laconic style, Pilar Quintana shows that she is one of the most powerful new voices of Latin America."
Deutschlandfunk Kultur

"This work is simple for the reader as far as the narrative is concerned; there are no far-fetched words or technicalities that complicate the reading. However, reading *The Bitch* is not easy at all because of the emotional load that Damaris's life represents, and with it the lives of thousands of women in Colombia and the world who make this fiction a sordid reality, people who ask, shouting, that we recognize them and make them visible."
Liberando Letras

"The central relationship of the story allows readers to learn about the harsh history of mistreatment, abandonment, injustice, and heartbreak suffered by the humble and kind Damaris. Thus, enduring the heavy humidity of the jungle that Quintana masterfully portrays, little by little the story makes readers look their own shadows in the eye. Perhaps, in this way, *The Bitch* is a mirror-novel: it invites us to look at what we are not, in order to recognize ourselves."
Radio Nacional de Colombia

"Quintana uses language in such a neat way—neat in the sense of its economy—that her novel, in form if not in substance, could be compared to *The Old Man and the Sea*. The dogs in Quintana's novel are similar to the dogs in such relevant novels by José Saramago as *The Stone Raft*, *The Cave*, and *Blindness*, works in which dogs become characters, even protagonists—in this sense Quintana's novel is similar to that of the Portuguese writer."

Hecho en Cali

ABYSS

PILAR QUINTANA

ABYSS

Translated from the Spanish
by Lisa Dillman

WORLD EDITIONS
New York, London, Amsterdam

Property of Gloucester County Library

Published in the USA in 2023 by World Editions LLC, New York
Published in the UK in 2023 by World Editions Ltd., London

World Editions
New York | London | Amsterdam

First published as *Los abismos* in Spain
Copyright © Pilar Quintana / Penguin Random House Grupo
Editorial, S.A.U., 2021
English translation copyright © Lisa Dillman, 2023
Author portrait © Danilo Costa

Printed by Lake Book, USA
World Editions is committed to a sustainable future. Papers used
by World Editions meet the FSC standards of certification.

This book is a work of fiction. Any resemblance to actual persons,
living or dead, or actual events is purely coincidental.

Library of Congress Cataloging in Publication Data is available

ISBN 978-1-64286-122-8

All rights reserved. No part of this publication may be reproduced,
stored in or introduced into a retrieval system, or transmitted, in
any form, or by any means (electronic, mechanical, photocopying,
recording or otherwise) without the prior written permission of the
publisher.

Twitter: @WorldEdBooks
Facebook: @WorldEditionsInternationalPublishing
Instagram: @WorldEdBooks
YouTube: World Editions
www.worldeditions.org

For my sisters

"My soul hurls itself into a revolting black abyss, viscous, that enters my mouth, my ears, my nose."

Fernando Iwasaki, "The Stranger"

PART ONE

THERE WERE SO many plants in the apartment that we called it the jungle.

The building looked like something out of an old futurist movie. Flat lines, overhangs, lots of gray, wide open spaces, huge windows. Our apartment was two stories, and the living-room window went all the way from the bottom of the first floor to the top of the second. Downstairs, the floor tiles were black granite with white veins. Upstairs, white granite with black veins. The staircase had black steel tubes and polished slabs for steps. A naked staircase, full of holes. The upstairs hall overlooked the living room, like a balcony, and had the same tube railing as the stairs. From there you could gaze down at the jungle below, sprawling in all directions.

There were plants on the floor and on tables, on top of the hi-fi and the buffet, between pieces of furniture, on wrought iron stands and in ceramic pots, hanging from the walls and ceiling on the staircase's lowest steps, and in places you couldn't see from the upstairs: the kitchen, the laundry room, the guest bathroom. All kinds of plants. Sun, shade, water. A few, like red anthurium and white egret, had flowers. The rest were green. Ferns both smooth and curly, shrubs with striped leaves, spotted leaves, colorful leaves, palms, bushes, huge trees that grew well in planters, and delicate herbs that fit into my small hand.

Sometimes, walking through the apartment, I had the feeling the plants were reaching out with their finger-leaves, trying to touch me; and that the biggest ones, in a forest behind the three-seater sofa, liked to envelop the people sitting there or brush up against them and cause a fright.

Out on the street, two guayacanes obstructed the view from the balcony and living room. In the rainy season, their leaves fell off and the trees became covered in pink flowers. Birds would hop from the guayacanes onto the balcony. Hummingbirds and tropical kingbirds—the most intrepid—would pop in to nose around. Butterflies would flutter fearlessly from the dining room to the living room. Sometimes, at night, a bat would get in and fly around, low to the ground, looking lost. Mamá and I would scream. Papá would grab a broom and stand, motionless, in the middle of the jungle until the bat flew out the way it had come in.

In the afternoons a cool wind came down from the hills and swept over Cali. It stirred the guayacanes, blew in through the open windows, and rustled the indoor plants too. The racket it made sounded like people at a concert. In the afternoons, mamá watered. Water overflowed pots, filtered down through the dirt, seeped out the holes, and dripped onto the ceramic plates, trickling like a little stream.

I loved running through the jungle, letting the plants caress me, stopping in their midst, closing my eyes and listening to their sounds. The tinkle of water, the whisper of air, the nervous, agitated branches. I loved running up the stairs and looking down from the second floor, as if at the edge of a cliff, the stairs a fractured ravine. Our jungle, lush and savage, down below.

Mamá was always home. She didn't want to be like my grandmother. She spent her whole life telling me so.

My grandmother slept till midmorning, so my mother had to go to school without seeing her. In the afternoons, my grandmother played lulo with her friends, meaning that four days out of five, when mamá got home from school her mother wasn't there. The one day she was, it was because it was her turn to host the card game. Eight ladies at the dining room table, smoking, laughing, tossing down cards and eating pandebono cheese bread. My grandmother didn't even look at mamá.

One time, at the club, mamá heard a woman ask my grandmother why she hadn't had more children.

"Ay, mija," my grandmother said, "if I could have avoided it, I wouldn't even have had this one."

The two of them burst out laughing. My mother had just gotten out of the pool and was standing there dripping water. It felt, she said, like they'd ripped open her chest and reached in to tear out her heart.

My grandfather got back from work in the evening. He'd hug mamá, tickle her, ask about her day. But apart from that, she grew up in the care of maids, who came and went, one after the other, since my grandmother never liked any of them.

Maids didn't last long at our house.

Yesenia was from the Amazon jungle. She was

nineteen, with straight hair down to her waist and the rough-hewn features of the stone sculptures at San Agustín. We hit it off from the first day.

My school was a few blocks from our apartment building. Yesenia would walk me there in the mornings and be waiting for me when I got out in the afternoons. On the way, she'd tell me about where she was from. The fruits, the animals, the rivers wider than an avenue.

"That," she said, pointing to Cali River, "is not a river; it's a creek."

One afternoon we went straight to her bedroom. A small room off the kitchen, with a bathroom and a tiny window. We sat facing each other on her bed. We'd discovered that she didn't know any songs or hand games, and I was teaching her my favorite one, about dolls from Paris. She was getting it all wrong, and we were laughing our heads off. My mother appeared in the doorway.

"Claudia, come upstairs."

She looked super serious.

"What's wrong?"

"I said: *come*."

"We were just playing."

"Do not make me repeat myself."

I looked at Yesenia. With her eyes, she told me to obey. I stood up and went. Mamá grabbed my schoolbag off the floor. We climbed the stairs, went into my room, and she closed the door.

"Never again do I want to see you getting friendly with her."

"With Yesenia?"

"With any maid."

"But why?"

"Because, my girl, she's the maid."

"Why does that matter?"

"Because you get attached to them and then they leave."

"Yesenia doesn't know anybody in Cali. She can stay with us forever."

"Ay, Claudia, don't be so naive."

A few days later, Yesenia left without saying goodbye while I was at school.

My mother said she'd gotten a call from her hometown of Leticia, and had to return to her family. I suspected it was untrue, but mamá stuck to her story.

Next came Lucila, an older woman from the Cauca region who paid no attention to me and was the maid who stayed with us the longest.

Mamá did her housewife things in the mornings, when I was at school. The shopping, the errands, the bills. At lunchtime she picked my father up from the supermarket and they had lunch together at the apartment. Then in the afternoons he drove back to work, and she stayed home to wait for me.

When I got home from school, I'd find her in bed with a magazine. She liked ¡Hola!, Vanidades, and Cosmopolitan. There, she read about the lives of famous women. The articles came accompanied by large color photos of houses, yachts, and parties. I ate lunch and she turned pages. I did homework and she turned pages. At four o'clock, the only TV station began its daily programming, and as I watched Sesame Street she turned pages.

Mamá once told me that shortly before graduating

from high school she'd waited for my grandfather to come home from work, to tell him that she wanted to go to university. They were in my grandparents' bedroom. He took off his guayabera, let it drop to the floor, and stood there in his undershirt. Big and hairy, with his taut round belly. A bear. Then he stared at her with strange-looking eyes she didn't recognize.

"Law," my mother dared to add.

My grandfather's neck veins bulged, and in his gruffest voice he told her that what decent señoritas did was get married: *university, law, his foot*! His furious voice booming as if through a megaphone. I could practically hear it as my mother, just a girl, cowered and backed away.

Less than a month later he had a heart attack and died.

In the study, we had a wall where family portraits hung.

The one of my maternal grandparents was a black-and-white photo in a silver frame. It had been taken at the club's New Year's party, the last one my maternal grandparents had spent together. Streamers fell all around, people wore paper hats and held party blowers. My grandparents were just emerging from an embrace. Laughing. Him: a giant in a tux, bifocals, drink in hand. You couldn't see his hair, but I knew, from other photos and from my mother, that it sprouted out from everywhere. His shirtsleeves, his back, his nose, even his ears. My grandmother was in an elegant, open-back dress, with a cigarette holder between her fingers and a bouffant hairdo.

She was long and skinny, an upright worm. Beside him she looked diminutive.

Beauty and the Beast, I always thought, though my mother would defend her father, saying he was no beast, he was a teddy bear and only got mad that one time.

My grandfather worked his whole life in the sales department of an electrical appliance factory. He had big clients, earned a good salary, and made commissions on every sale. After he died there were no more commissions, and the pension my grandmother received was a fraction of his salary.

My grandmother and mother were forced to sell the car, the club membership, and the house in San Fernando. They moved to a rental apartment in town, fired the live-in maids and hired one who went home at the end of the day. They stopped going to the beauty parlor and learned to do their own nails and hair. My grandmother's was a short beehive, which she teased with a comb, using half a can of hairspray until it was piled up high. She forwent her lulo games, since hosting eight women every time it was her turn to entertain was too costly, and took up canasta, which was played with only four.

Mamá, fresh out of high school, began volunteering at San Juan de Dios Hospital, an activity grandfather would have approved of.

San Juan de Dios was a charity hospital. I never saw the inside but pictured it as filthy and dismal, with bloodstained walls and moribund patients groaning in the hallways. One day when I said so out loud, my mother laughed. Actually, she said, it was airy and luminous, with white walls and interior courtyards. A 1700s building, well taken care of by the nuns who ran it.

That was where she met my father.

My paternal grandparents' portrait was oval, in a bronze openwork frame. They lived before my other grandparents' time, in an age my child's mind pictured to be as dark as the colors of the portrait.

This one was an oil painting of their wedding day, copied from a studio photograph, with a brown background and opaque details. The bride was the only luminous thing in it. A girl of sixteen. She was sitting on a wooden chair. Her wedding dress covered her from neck to shoes. She wore a mantilla and a demure smile, and held a rosary in her hands. It looked like she was getting confirmed, like the groom was really her father. He stood, one hand on her shoulder, like an old wooden post. A brittle man, bald, in a gray suit and thick glasses.

My grandmother, that girl, was not yet even twenty when she died giving birth to my father. They lived on my grandfather's coffee farm. Grandfather moved to Cali. Devastated by the loss, I assumed. A forlorn man in no state to take care of anyone. The newborn and his sister, my tía Amelia, who was two, stayed on the farm and were cared for by a sister of the deceased.

Tía Amelia and my father were raised on that farm. When the time came, their aunt enrolled them at the local school, where the children of peasants and workers went. In second grade, when their shoes got too small, the aunt hacked off the tips with a knife and they went to class with their toes poking out.

"Were they poor?"

This was my tía that I was asking; she's the one who told me the story.

"Ha! Not in the slightest. The farm was prosperous."

"Then why didn't they buy you new shoes?"

"Who knows," she said, then paused and added, "my father never visited us."

"Because he was sad about your mother's death?"

"No doubt."

The aunt fell ill. There was nothing the doctors could do, and after she died the children were sent to be with their father in Cali. He sold the coffee farm and opened the supermarket.

Tía Amelia and my father lived with my grandfather until they were grown up. He developed emphysema, since he smoked two packs a day, and died long before my time. That was when the two of them inherited the supermarket.

My tía Amelia knew everything that went on at the supermarket, but she didn't work there. She spent all day at the apartment in a housedress, cigarette in hand, with a glass of wine if it was night. She had housedresses in every style and color. Mexican, Guajiran, Indian, tie-dyed, Cartago embroidered.

Whenever her birthday or Christmas was coming up, my mother would complain that she didn't know what to get her. In the end, she'd give her a housedress. My aunt always received the gift with what seemed like authentic joy and said that she loved it, that she didn't have this style, or that this precise color was exactly what she needed.

My father was the supermarket manager. He never took vacations. The only time he wasn't working was when the supermarket was closed, on Sundays and holidays. He was the first to arrive in the morning, the last to leave in the evening, and sometimes had to go in to receive delayed shipments in the middle of the night. Saturdays, after closing, he used to go to San Juan de Dios Hospital to donate groceries for the infirm.

My mother was in the pantry, making space for the newly arrived food, when my father turned up. She didn't notice him. He, on the other hand, was so taken that he went to ask the nun in charge who she was. The nun, in mamá's words, was short and squat. The stump of a felled tree, that was how I pictured her, brown habit flaring at the bottom.

"The new volunteer," she told my father. "Her name is Claudia."

He and the nun stood gazing at my mother.

"And she's single," she added.

Perhaps that was what gave him courage. My father waited until she finished her shift. He approached, introduced himself, and offered to accompany her home. She, all of nineteen, looked him up and down and saw a forty-something-year-old man.

"No, thank you," she replied.

My father didn't give up. He'd turn up at the hospital with chocolates, pistachios, or some other delicacy he'd bought at La Cristalina, a shop that sold fancy imported goods. Mamá refused his gifts.

"Jorge," she said one day, "are you never going to grow tired of this?"

"No."

She laughed.

"I brought you Danish butter cookies."

They came in a big tin and my mother couldn't resist. She took it.

"So, today do I get to accompany you home?"

This time she couldn't say no.

My grandmother adored this gallant gentleman with a good inheritance who practiced Christian charity, donating groceries to the hospital.

"He's an old man," my mother pointed out.

"I thought you liked older men?"

This was true. Mamá couldn't stand boys her own age, a bunch of dimwits in her view, who spent all day horsing around in the pool at the club.

"Not *that* old," she said.

My grandmother rolled her eyes.

"Claudia, you're impossible."

The following Monday when my mother got home from the hospital, she found the canasta ladies at the house, shrouded in a cloud of cigarette smoke and eating Danish butter cookies. Four housewives with hairdos big as balloons and long painted fingernails, which they used to deal and spread their cards across the table.

It was terribly hot, my mother said. That terrible Cali heat, I thought, the kind that laid you out flat. The women led her to a seat, and she sat. Aída de Solanilla took a cookie and savored it.

"At forty," she said once she'd swallowed, "a man's not old; he's in the prime of life."

"He's twenty-one years older than me," my mother said.

Her own husband, Aída said, was eighteen years older; Lola de Aparicio's was twenty; Miti de Villalobos, who wasn't there but was a friend from their lulo days, had married a man twenty-five years older; and all three could attest to the fact that their marriages were as good as any could be, better than those between same-age spouses, where both bride and groom are young and rash.

The women turned to my mother. She contended that the man wore bottleneck glasses and was bald, short, and too skinny.

"Jorge is very dapper," Aída de Solanilla countered. "I see him at the supermarket all the time. His clothes are expensive, well ironed."

My mother couldn't deny this.

"But he barely speaks," she said.

"Ay, mija," Lola de Aparicio retorted, opening her Spanish fan. "If you spend your life finding fault with every man you meet, you'll end up alone."

My grandmother and the other women nodded, staring at mamá. That terrible heat, I felt it, like a rope around her neck.

In my mother's day, it was tradition for the parents of the bride to bear the cost of the wedding. But to my grandmother's delight and relief, papá wouldn't let her pay a single peso, and he let my mother plan it however she wished.

She didn't want any parties, just a church ceremony. Her dress was white, though not exactly a bridal gown—a plain, knee-length dress with no veil—and she wore her hair in a simple bun, with a comb decorated with tiny flowers. My father was in a morning coat, just like his father in the photo, but older and balder.

The photo of my parents on the wall was black and white, in a wood frame. They were at the altar. The priest, the table, and Christ in the background. The bride and groom up front, facing one another, exchanging rings. He was beaming. She, her eyes cast down, looked sad, but that was because she was concentrating on putting on his ring.

Two weeks later my grandmother died of a brain hemorrhage.

At first the newlyweds lived in a rented apartment. My grandfather's house was too big for my tía Amelia, so they sold it and used the money to buy two apartments. A small one for my tía in Portada al Mar, at the foot of the mountain, a few blocks from the supermarket and on the edge of a traditional neighborhood with both grand old houses and new apartment buildings. The other, for my parents, very nearby, in the twinned neighborhood on the other side of the river.

The previous owners of my parents' apartment had left a plant on the balcony. A spider plant with long, white-rimmed leaves. The tips were burned and the colors faded. My grandmother had one like it at the house in San Fernando, back before my grandfather died and she and mamá had to upend their lives. Mamá, who was still mourning both their deaths, adopted it.

The dining room had wood-framed folding glass doors that opened out onto the balcony. My mother brought the spider plant inside. She watered it, transplanted it into a big pot, gave it fresh soil. Never before had mamá been responsible for a living thing and she was delighted when it turned green.

Seeing her joy, Doña Imelda, the cashier at the supermarket, gave her the offshoot of a Swiss cheese plant. Mamá planted it in a clay pot and put it on the coffee table. The cheese plant spilled down toward the floor. Then my father brought her a maidenhair fern, and tía Amelia, for her birthday, gave her a miniature umbrella tree.

Slowly the apartment began filling with plants, until it turned into the jungle. I always thought of the plants as my mother's dead. Her dead, reborn.

The earliest memory I have is of me on the stairs. Me, behind a child-proof safety gate at the long, broken stairs: an impossible cliff down to the wonderful green world of the first floor.

My second memory is of being on my parents' bed. Me and my mother, her with her magazine, me jumping.

"Mamamamamamamama."

Suddenly the explosion.

"Dammit, child! Can't you be still?!"

Or maybe that was before the stairs and it only feels more recent because I relived it so many times.

Mamá in bed with her magazine, and me lifting her shirt to blow bubbles on her tummy.

"Must you be all over me all the time?"

Me planting little kisses on her arm.

"Leave me in peace for just one minute, Claudia, for God's sake."

Gazing at her as she combs her hair at the dressing table. Long and straight, the color of chocolate, hair that made you want to stroke it.

"Why don't you go to your room?"

Me, bigger, climbing onto her bed when I finished my homework.

"Hi, mamá."

Her, clearly annoyed, getting up and leaving me on her bed with the open magazine.

"Why did you stop working at the hospital?" I asked.

"Because I got married."

"And after you got married you didn't want to go to university anymore?"

She went to say something but then stopped.

"Papá wouldn't let you?"

"It's not that."

"What then?"

"I didn't even ask him."

"You didn't want to?"

"I would have liked to, yes."

"So why didn't you?"

She closed the magazine. It was an *¡Hola!* On the cover, Carolina of Monaco in a strapless ball gown, with real rubies and diamonds.

"Because you were born."

She got up and walked out into the hall. I followed.

"Why didn't you have more children?"

"Another pregnancy? Another childbirth? A crying baby? Ay, no. No, thank you. Not for me. Besides, my body got damaged more than enough just with you."

"If you could have avoided it, you wouldn't have had me?"

She stopped and gazed at me.

"Oh, Claudia, I'm not like my mother."

My birthday fell over the long school holiday, on Independence Day, when there were parades and people were out of town at their country houses or the beach. We could only celebrate with family, so we went to a restaurant.

My mother, as she did each year, recounted her pregnancy. Her giant belly, her swollen feet, how every five minutes she had to go to the bathroom, how she couldn't sleep and struggled to get out of bed. The pains had started around lunchtime. They were the most awful thing she'd ever felt. Papá took her to the clinic, where she agonized all afternoon, all night, all the next morning, and all that afternoon, feeling like she was about to die, and then another whole night and into the early morning hours.

"She came out purple. Hideous. They put her on my chest, shaking and crying, and I thought: all that effort for this?"

And mamá laughed so wide you could see the roof of her mouth, hollow and grooved like an underfed torso.

"Ugliest baby in the clinic," said papá.

He and tía Amelia laughed too, showing tongues, teeth, half-chewed food.

"The other baby born that day was beautiful," my tía said.

The last photo on the study wall was from the day I was born. A rectangle, like the portrait of my maternal grandparents, black and white and in a silver frame.

My mother, in bed at the clinic with me in her arms, showed no signs of suffering. Her hair was done, eyes lined, lips glossed and smiling. My aunt and father, standing on either side of the bed, were smiling too. She was in a bell-sleeved dress with arabesque motifs and had a mushroom bob with one corkscrew curl hanging down to her chin. Papá had long sideburns, his bald head less bare back then. I was a blanket-wrapped blob. A tiny thing with black hair and swollen eyes.

"Am I still ugly?"

We were in the study. My father was reading the paper in his recliner. Mamá was pruning the bonsai, the only plant on the second floor.

"What are you talking about?" she asked, as if she didn't know.

"You were joking today about how ugly I was when I was born."

"All newborns are ugly."

"Tía Amelia said the other baby was beautiful."

Papá laughed out loud.

"Don't laugh!" I screamed. And to mamá, "Am I still ugly?"

She put her shears down, came over and crouched down to my height.

"You're beautiful."

"Tell me the truth."

"Claudia, there are some women whose beauty doesn't show till they are older, when they develop. At your age, I was short, dark, and scrawny too. You've seen the photo albums, haven't you?"

I had, of course, but that didn't help at all because the only thing we had in common was our name. The rest of me took after my father. Everyone said so; we were identical.

"Don't you know the story of the ugly duckling?" she asked. And that was worse.

My father's birthday, ten days after mine, was the last time the four of us—tía Amelia, my parents, and me—were alone together. We celebrated at our apartment. The jungle decorated with streamers, a big sign I made, and an orange cake my tía had baked. Mamá and I gave papá a new radio for his office. My tía handed him a box wrapped in silver paper from Zas, a department store at the mall. Inside was an elegant light-blue Italian shirt.

Soon after that my aunt took a trip to Europe. We assumed she was going on a tour with two old school friends, like when she traveled around South America or went to see the Mayan ruins. Mamá thought it was odd that she didn't want us to take her to the airport or pick her up, but she wasn't even close to guessing why.

WHEN SHE GOT back from her trip, tía Amelia called to invite us to lunch at whatever restaurant I wanted. I picked El Búho de Humo, the Smoke Owl, because I liked their pizza and the tables with long benches like out of an American movie.

It was a dark place. Blue neon from the sign filtered in through the window. My aunt was at the back, with a man we didn't know. As soon as they saw us they stood. He was young and muscly, with a matador's waist, his butt sausaged into his pants, and a TV-star hairstyle.

"Let me introduce you to Gonzalo, my husband."

My parents stood there as if someone had yelled "Freeze!" I was excited, but for a different reason. Sitting on the table, like a real little girl, was a doll.

"What's that doll?"

She had long chocolate-brown hair, exactly like my mother's, a green velvet dress, white socks folded down at the ankle, and patent-leather shoes.

"Who do you think it's for?" my tía asked.

"Me?"

"That's right, young lady," Gonzalo confirmed. "We bought her in Madrid. She didn't fit in our suitcase, so we had to hold her hand for the whole rest of the trip."

"Like a crippled daughter," tía Amelia said laughing. "In London we nearly left her at the airport."

I picked her up. She had a tiny little nose, lips puckered into a pinch, bright blue eyes like two miniature planet Earths, and eyelids that opened and closed and had long lashes that looked like real hair.

"I can't believe she's mine."

I hugged the dolly and my aunt.

"Her name is Paulina. Isn't she pretty?"

"The prettiest doll ever."

I sat with Paulina between my legs. The adults remained standing. My parents, still flabbergasted.

"You got married?" my mother asked.

"At Segunda Notary, the day before our trip."

"Well ... congratulations."

Mamá hugged my tía and kissed Gonzalo. Now it was my father's turn. Unsure what to do, he smiled. Gonzalo held out a hand. Papá shook it and then kissed his sister.

"You certainly kept that under wraps," said my mother after they sat down.

Tía Amelia and Gonzalo laughed. She told us she'd met him at Zas the day she went to buy my father's birthday present.

"He showed me the shirts and we just couldn't stop talking."

"Luckily," he said, "she left me a piece of paper with her phone number before walking out."

"The birthday ... two months ago?" my mother asked.

"Yep," Gonzalo replied. "It was all so fast."

My parents looked at one another. My aunt lit a cigarette and as she inhaled little wrinkles appeared above her top lip, like rivers on a map.

We walked out of El Búho de Humo, me happily carrying Paulina. Tía Amelia and Gonzalo carried on to her car, a Renault 6 everyone said was blue but looked green to me. We got into ours, a mustard-yellow Renault 12.

The second we closed the car doors, my mother said quietly, in the voice she used when she thought it best for me not to hear: "She could have just been his girlfriend, no?"

Papá started the car.

"She was very lonely."

"But she didn't have to get married so quickly."

Papá looked over his shoulder. I was facing backwards, crouching on the little hump that Renault 12s had on the floor, with my new dolly standing up on the back seat. I pretended to be playing rather than paying attention. He turned back around: "The guy took advantage of her weakness."

The car began moving.

"She was the one who left him her number, asked him to marry her, and invited him on the trip. In case you didn't hear her."

"Mija, it's clear he's a hustler."

My father never talked bad like that about anyone.

"What makes it clear?"

"You can tell."

"By his face?" asked mamá.

"Amelia is fifty-one, this guy's not even thirty."

"And that makes him a hustler?"

We'd reached the main road, headlights from all the moving cars crisscrossed the darkness in every direction.

"Do you honestly think he's in love with her?" he asked.

"No, and that's why she shouldn't have been in

such a hurry. But I also don't think she's some poor victim, or that he tricked her or is taking advantage of her. More like they have an arrangement that works for both of them."

"Works for both of them! Did you see who paid the bill?"

Now it was my mother who turned around. I was making Paulina talk to me, using a high-pitched girlie voice, and then answering her in my real voice.

"And who do you expect to pay the bills?" she retorted. "Him? With his Zas-salesboy salary?"

"He needs to sign a document stipulating that he inherits nothing and ends up with nothing if they divorce."

An icy silence ensued. Carefully, I turned to face forward. Mamá was staring at papá like she couldn't believe what he'd just said. He sat there, rigid, hands tight on the wheel.

"What?" he said. "Is it wrong that I want to protect my sister, and the family inheritance?"

"Jorge, I'm twenty-eight and you're forty-nine ..."

"That's different," he said.

Indignant, my mother stared straight ahead; neither of them said another word.

On Sunday we went to tía Amelia's for a visit. Gonzalo opened the door. He was in shorts and a tank top, with his hair recently blow-dried and his muscles all puffed out. She was sitting on her wicker chair, a cigarette in one hand and a glass of wine in the other, in a white housedress with billowy sleeves that flapped like wings when she got up and spread her arms wide in greeting.

A gust of wind blew in from the balcony. The curtains billowed up and the bedroom door slammed. Gonzalo reopened it and wedged it with a conch, and we saw there were now two beds.

"Hey, I thought you got married," I said.

"They *are* married," my mother replied, clenching her teeth so I'd be quiet.

"Then why do you sleep separate?"

"Don't be imprudent, Claudia."

My aunt laughed. "Because I don't like anybody stealing the blanket."

She set her wineglass down on the table and gave me a hug.

Other novelties at the apartment included two dumbbells and a basket of magazines by the bathroom door. The house had no TV, no toys, and no pets, and therefore nothing to do. I sat Paulina on the floor and began flipping through the magazines. All *Popular Mechanics*: boring, boring, boring. The articles were about cars and machines. There were instructions on how to build an airplane at home, tips on lawnmower maintenance.

I was about to give up on them when I came across one with a naked lady on the cover. On her back, with her body turned slightly forward. She had a naughty expression on her face and a see-through shawl that covered her torso but not her bottom or boobies. It was a *Playboy*.

María del Carmen, my friend from school, had told me her brother had a *Playboy* hidden under his mattress and that she looked at it. I'd never been this close to one, much less held it in my hands.

Papá and tía Amelia were going through an account log in the dining room. Mamá and Gonzalo were talking in the living room. Her back was to the bathroom. He was the only one who'd seen what I was doing. He set his wineglass on the table, leaned over to my mother and said something. She turned.

"Claudia, put that down and come here."

"But ..."

"But nothing," she said using the voice that meant you better obey.

The next time we visited I spent my time wandering the apartment in silence, acting absentminded until I got my hands on the *Playboy*. I locked myself in the bathroom with it. Before I could even get past the advertisements on the first few pages there was knocking on the door.

"What are you doing, Claudia?"

It was my mother.

"Nothing."

"Open the door please."

"Coming."

"This instant."

She confiscated the *Playboy*, put it back in the basket, and took me into the living room with her.

On our third visit I waited until they were all distracted before sitting on the floor by the basket and hunting through the *Popular Mechanics* until I got to the *Playboy*. My father and aunt were talking in the living room. My mother and Gonzalo were pouring the wine in the kitchen. I took the magazine and opened it. Finally, I managed to see the photos of naked women and read the captions. *Some women are animals in bed.*

From where my father and aunt were, you couldn't see the kitchen. From where I was, you could. Gonzalo and mamá were talking, laughing, toasting, and for a minute they looked at each other in silence. He, facing the door, saw me and said something to mamá. She walked out of the kitchen, wineglass in hand, pretending to be mad when she couldn't have been happier.

"What are you doing, Claudia?"

"Gonzalo told me they have aerobics classes at his gym," mamá said.

We were in the car. Her in the passenger seat, papá at the wheel.

"The teacher is French. They say she's marvelous."

I was in the back seat, Paulina beside me.

"There's a class on Saturday mornings."

There were no people out, no cars on the tree-lined avenue, just samans and ceibas. Besides us, only the river was in motion.

"It's for women, women my age and older go."

Since my father wasn't saying anything, my mother stopped talking.

Cali—split in two by a curving stone-filled river, its low buildings set among trees taller than they were—resembled a lost city.

"Do you two want an ice cream on a stick?" my father asked.

"Yes!" I screamed, excited.

Mamá said nothing.

"You don't want one?" he asked.

She made a face that meant she didn't care one way or the other. He tried to tempt her.

"How about a nice blackberry one?"

Mamá sat there, stiff and mute, like a second Paulina. We were all silent. Every little while he'd glance over at her.

"Would you like to go to the aerobics class?" he said finally.

She looked at him.

"Well, I am curious about it, yes, but I wouldn't want to leave Claudia with the maid."

He patted her thigh a few times.

"Don't you worry, mija. I can take her with me to the supermarket."

Saturday morning my mother dropped us at the supermarket and drove to the gym. My father went into his office. I set about wandering the aisles, bored, trailing a finger across the merchandise until I came to the shelf with powdered jello. Unable to resist, I opened a box of grape. I was just licking the purple remains from the palm of my hand when Doña Imelda, the cashier, discovered me.

"I knew all that silence meant something."

Doña Imelda had elephant wrinkles on her face, jet-black hair, and thick arms. From a distance, in her light green uniform, she looked like a nurse straight out of some horror movie.

"Would you like a little job, sweetheart?"

From up close, she was sweet and affectionate.

"Yes, please," I said.

"Do you think you could wipe those cans down?"

The rack was overflowing with them, top to bottom. Doña Imelda handed me a rag and gave me a triangle ladder so I could reach the highest shelves and then went back to the register. The task took ages and the cans ended up all nice and clean, but uneven. Doña Imelda showed me how to line them up, and then I left them really perfect. Next she had me sort through packs of toilet paper. By the time I finished, the supermarket had closed for lunch.

Papá and Doña Imelda began talking about the orders they needed to place. We walked out through the back door with the stock boy. The two of them headed toward their neighborhood of bare-brick and tin-roof houses, in the slopes of the mountain.

"Isn't mamá coming to pick us up?"

"She called to say she was going to the sauna and would be late, so we should walk home and order a chicken. Lucila left early."

Papá took my hand. We crossed the street, walked down the block with the drug store and the bank, and waved to the lottery-ticket vendor standing on the corner, serving a customer. After we got to the intersection where the bridge crossed over the river and were halfway down the block, my father went over to a car stopped at a stop sign and practically stuck his head through the window.

"Hellooooo!"

I was so distracted I hadn't realized it was our Renault 12, with my mother inside, and was as startled as she was.

"Ay, Jorge, you startled me!"

We turned around and got in.

"You look lovely," he said.

The upholstery was black leather and hot as river

stones at midday, but mamá looked fresh and cool in her tight red bodysuit, with her hair all wet.

"I took a shower," she explained.

"What are you doing here?"

There was no reason for her to go through the supermarket neighborhood on her way home.

"I bumped into Gonzalo on my way out and gave him a ride."

"Oh."

"I didn't stop for you two because the doors were already closed so I assumed you'd left."

"It took us a while to get the orders together."

Mamá put her hand on the gearshift and pulled out. Papá, who couldn't stop staring at her, stroked her arm.

"Really, so lovely."

If I begged hard enough and she was in a good mood, my mother would let me sit at her dressing table.

"Don't go messing anything up, tocaya," she said. Tocaya: namesake. She sometimes called me that.

It was an antique vanity she'd inherited from my grandmother, with a round mirror and several drawers full of hairbrushes, makeup brushes, jars, tubes, little boxes of powder, and assorted bottles. I was putting on red lipstick when she, from her bed, began to moan. She'd put down her magazine and was trying to stand up.

"Ay, ay, ay."

Everything hurt, from the aerobics. I finished with the lipstick, grabbed a green eyeshadow and began to apply it. In the mirror I watched as she hobbled to the bathroom, slow and stiff, like she was made of metal.

Contemplating myself, I looked at my face from this angle and that. Next I took a brush and put blusher on my cheeks. The phone rang. I went to answer.

"I'll get it, Claudiaaaaaa!" she screamed from the bathroom.

It rang again. Already at the night table, I picked up.

"Hello?"

There was breathing on the other end of the line.

The bathroom door opened.

"Hello? Hello?"

My mother rushed over as fast as she could and snatched the receiver from me.

"Hello?"

The person had hung up. Vexed, she put the receiver down and glared at me. The rage of the world was concentrated in her nose, nostrils flaring in and out.

"Look at that face," she snapped. "You look like a clown."

Since she was always in bed beside her night table, most of the time my mother was the one to answer the phone. I would guess who'd called by her tone of voice. The one she used for tía Amelia was the same as the one for Gloria Inés. She could talk for ages with either of them. The difference was that with Gloria Inés she laughed more. Gloria Inés was the daughter of one of my grandmother's second cousins. My mother's only remaining relative. If it was Doña Imelda, she used the formal *usted* and discussed plants. With my father she was direct, like with the bank advisor and the building manager, only more familiar.

Downstairs, there was another phone on the living-room side table. Sometimes me or Lucila would answer before she did.

"Hello?"

It became standard for the person on the other end of the line not to speak.

"Hello, hello."

And they'd hang up.

Sometimes, if I was downstairs running through the jungle and my mother was in her room, or the other way around, if she was down watering plants and I was leafing through one of her magazines, we'd pick up at the same time.

"Hello?"

Silence. Mamá would tell me to hang up and, when I did, the person talked. Whenever the mute called, mamá whispered and put on a soft voice.

Wednesday afternoons I had art class. I'd get home from school, eat lunch, and mamá would drive me to the academy. It was in the Granada neighborhood, in an old house with columns, mosaic tiles, and interior courtyards. Mamá would drive off and I'd go to my class, which lasted an hour and a half. When it was over she'd come back for me. We would stop at the supermarket, buy milk, eggs, bread, or whatever else we needed, paying like regular customers, and then my father would drop us back at the apartment and take the car back with him until closing time.

Sometimes, on other afternoons—like Fridays or when I didn't have school the next day—mamá and I would go to the shopping district, a series of stores close to Sears, on the streets of a neighborhood that had once been residential. We bought my mother's magazines at Librería Nacional. We window-shopped. The afternoon winds messed up our hair and if there were women in skirts, it would lift them up. We'd eat peach palm, green mango, gooseberries, snow cones, cheese pastries from Rincón de la Abuela, and soft-serve ice cream from Dari, which had tables out front. We'd sit and, as I licked my cone, mamá would jiggle her foot impatiently.

Catty-corner, on the other side of the street, was Zas. Before long, Gonzalo would come over, and if he didn't, when I finished my ice cream my mother would grab my hand and we'd cross the street, dodging cars like an Atari frogger.

The Zas shop window took up the whole facade, with its display of well-dressed mannequins with stiff hair and mustaches. From inside the store, Gonzalo would smile, finish with a customer, and emerge. Or sometimes we went in. He hardly noticed I was there or even said hi to me.

"Señorita," was all he'd say.

Mamá was the only thing he cared about. He got so close when talking to her that it was impossible for me to hear, and if he paid any attention to me it was just to make sure I wasn't touching anything.

The changing rooms were in the back, past the shoe section. Three-piece suits to one side. At the glass counter in the middle of the shop, where the cash register was, they had accessories, cufflinks, billfolds, key rings, stuff like that. In front of the register were the shirts and pants, belts and ties.

The racks there were bolted to the floor. Metal skeletons. I liked the one with the ties, which hung straight down and traveled around in a little loop until they made a full circle. There were ties in lots of colors, ties with different motifs. Orange, gray, blue, pink, solid, striped, spotted, and with weird shapes. It looked like a circus curtain.

While mamá and Gonzalo were talking, I got the urge to pull back that curtain of ties and see what lay behind. A world full of wonders: a funfair with cotton candy, an enchanted forest, the land at the end of the rainbow. But Gonzalo was on constant alert. The minute he saw what my fingers were itching to do, he elbowed mamá.

"Don't even think about touching those ties, young lady," she warned.

In the shopping district, there was another store called Género. They sold fabric, and most of the year it was boring. But in October they stocked Halloween costumes, and in December there were Christmas decorations and other imported wonders.

That year they had Adidas sneakers, the latest style. In the window display, a pair of blue suede ones with yellow stripes. We went in. They fit perfectly. Mamá checked the price tag and was horrified.

"That's robbery."

"It's because they're so pretty."

"They might be pretty, but those stripes aren't made of gold ..."

"Please."

"No."

"I'm begging you."

"Take them off."

"But I need them."

"Right now, Claudia."

Begrudgingly, I took them off.

"How about for a Christmas present?"

"No."

She snatched them from my hands and stuck them back in the display.

"Don't be mean."

"Put on your shoes."

"If you get them for me for Christmas you never have to get me anything ever again, not for my first communion, not when I pass all my classes and move up to fourth grade, not for my birthday."

"This is the second time I'm telling you: put on your shoes."

I grabbed my shoes.

"Look how old they are. They're about to fall apart."

"Claudia ..."

Mamá was using her getting-mad voice. I'd better obey. I put on my shoes and we walked out of the store. Those Adidas were the coolest thing in the display.

"Look at them. They're the most beautiful tennis shoes in the whole universe and no one in all of Cali has them."

"That's enough."

"I can't live without them."

"I'm going to lose my temper, young lady."

"Pretty please."

She stopped.

"I'm warning you, Claudia. You carry on like this and not only do you not get the shoes, you don't get anything at all."

"But …"

"Not for Christmas or for your first communion or for moving up to fourth grade or for your birthday. Got it?"

Things had escalated to the point where I really had to shut my mouth. I nodded and we carried on walking.

It had been so hot since noon that the whole city seemed to be melting. Mamá had little beads of sweat over her top lip and the hairline at my temples was soaked. Suddenly a paper fluttered up from the ground. Tree branches quivered and for a second everything else stood still. The cars, the people, the noise. In the whole of Cali there was nothing but that breeze.

We got to Dari. Reluctantly accepting that I wasn't going to get the Adidas, I ordered the same thing I always did: a vanilla cone. We walked out, me with my ice cream in hand. The wind, now gusting crazily, blew our hair up in the air. Before we even had time to sit down, Gonzalo had trotted over from across the street. Mamá's expression softened. She clasped her hair with one hand and held it there until he came over and they stood face to face.

Me and Gonzalo didn't even say hello. I sat down. Ignored them. Set about licking my ice cream, a delicate operation given that the wind was melting it and my hair was getting stuck in the cream. I worked my way to the cone, devoured it slowly, and when there was nothing left, took my mother's hand.

"Are we going?"

She looked at me. Not a trace of the angry woman. We walked back through the shopping district. I assumed we were going to the car. Before I knew it, we were standing in front of Género.

"Are you going to buy them for me?"

I couldn't believe it.

"I'm going to buy them for you," she said, "as part of your Christmas presents."

The Christmas tree they had at Zas was gigantic. With a gold star on top. And red and silver balls that distorted my reflection, giving me dark extraterrestrial eyes, a squashed fig nose, a huge head, and a dwarf body. I wanted to show my mother. Neither she nor Gonzalo were nearby. I looked around and found them in the back, slipping into a changing room.

I wandered around the store, unsure what to do. One salesclerk was showing a customer some suits. Another was shining the shoes on display. The cashier, at his glass counter, was on the phone. And under the changing-room door, two pairs of shoes, Gonzalo's brown loafers and my mother's red heels, braided together.

I found myself back at the tie rack. The circus curtain, the worlds of wonders. A funfair, an enchanted forest, a magical land. The customer, the salesmen, and the cashier were still busy. I could have wandered out into the street, could have gotten lost in the city, could have been taken by a child snatcher or a crazy person or the bogeyman.

My hand was mucky with ice cream, fingers black and sticky. I looked in the wall mirror, saw my T-shirt with dribbles all down it, my face grimy, my ribbons twisted, hair tangled. A scarecrow. Puny and skinny and dark, like my mother said she was as a girl, but I looked exactly like my father. An ugly girl.

I returned to the curtain and its wonderful worlds. Softly, I ran my hand along the ties and they got messed up. I slipped my hands in and pulled the ties apart; the curtain separated. What a disappointment to find no cotton candy, no gnomes, no rainbow. Just a metal rack.

As revenge, I walked into the shirt display. My entire body in an ocean of seaweed. I hoped the whole thing would get dirty. Next I went inside a pants display, a stiff dark forest. And I didn't care if all the pants got ruined. I came out. The cashier hung up. The salesclerk was still with his suit customer. The other clerk still with the shoes. Mamá and Gonzalo still in the changing room.

I walked toward it. Stopped right in front of the door. Brown loafers facing red heels. The cashier came up beside me, smiled and held out a fist. He opened it. In his palm were some of the little red candies they offered customers.

"How long has it been since we've gone on vacation?" my mother asked.

My father made an I-don't-know face.

"A thousand million years," I said.

"Amelia was the one who made me realize. It would be so nice to go to La Bocana with them."

"I want to go to La Bocana!"

"We can't," said papá.

"Because of the supermarket," said mamá. "Always the same story. Work, work, work."

"That's life, what can I do?"

"Amelia agrees that we should close. It would be five days."

"No."

"Gonzalo got time off from Zas."

"Amelia told you that?"

"She did."

"Well I'm happy for them, but I can't close at the end of the year."

"We'll be on holiday hours already anyway, closing at lunch. So, actually it would only mean closing for five half-days."

"Booze sales over the holidays are the biggest all year."

My mother sighed. "I know."

We kept eating. The jungle around us was at peace. The evening air swaying it gently as though putting it to sleep. In the highest corner of the living room was a nocturnal butterfly. Impossible to reach. Even with the long window-cleaning poles. It had its wings spread, and big black eyes, and was stuck to the wall.

"It's going to attack us," I said.

"What is?" my mother asked.

"That butterfly."

"Ick, I hadn't seen it. It's enormous."

"It's gone," I said the next night when we sat down to dinner.

"What is?" my mother asked.

"The butterfly."

"Oh, I'd forgotten about it."

She had just finished dishing out soup.

"I found the solution," she said to my father.

"To what?"

"Our vacation."

"Mija ..."

"There's no need to close. Doña Imelda will look after things."

"She can't."

"'Go, have a good time,' she said."

"You already talked to her?"

My mother nodded.

"And Gloria Inés. She'll keep an eye on Doña Imelda, and stop by at closing every day to make sure everything is okay."

"What does Gloria Inés know about supermarkets?"

"Her husband's an economist."

"What does that have to do with anything?"

"Oh, Jorge, you're just *looking* for ways to throw a wrench in it all. The supermarket is the only thing that matters to you. It's never us. Never having a good time. Never getting out of this city. I want to travel, have a change of scenery, see new places, do different things. You're such a stick-in-the-mud."

"Can I bring Paulina?"

"No," my mother said. "We don't want her swept off by the sea, now, do we—or do we?"

It was always about to rain in La Bocana, and everything was gray. The sky, the sea, the sand, and the wood cabins up on stilts like street performers. The one we rented was two stories tall, on a hill called El Morro, which means the snout.

In the morning we'd go to the beach. My mother and aunt would sunbathe, reading mamá's magazines. I'd play in the sand with my father or with other kids, both local ones and tourists. Gonzalo would swim, jog, do calisthenics, and stride down the beach with his muscles popping out. He wore a tiny tanga and you could see his ding-dong through the fabric. And without his blow-dryer his hair was sparse and frizzy.

When tide came in, the beach shrank. We'd have fried fish or sancocho or shrimp with rice for lunch at one of the seaside shacks. Then the adults would sit around drinking beer and I'd go back to the sea and the other kids.

When tide went out, the beach grew big again. We'd paw through the things the sea had dragged in: seedpods, shells, bottles, starfish. Once I found a lucky rabbit's foot. It was all sandy and disgusting and I threw it away.

We knew it was time to go when the horrible clouds of midges flew in from the jungle, attacking us in swarms, biting through our clothes as we hurried to put them on, getting into our ears and eyes and noses.

At night, ferocious storms lashed down. There was no electricity in La Bocana. We used kerosene lamps for light, and they let off smoke and attracted moths and nocturnal butterflies. Some were beautiful, with delicate colors and yellow fuzz on their feet. Others were dark and terrifying, a thousand times bigger than the one in our apartment.

We'd get out the cards and play, using dried beans to make bets. Playing in silence, smiling the same calm smile as always, my father fleeced us. The adults would be drinking. Wine, rum, aguardiente. We'd laugh and my aunt would wobble off to bed.

My parents and I slept in the same room. Them in a double bed and me in a single, with a nightstand in between. Getting ready for bed, and seeing mine all empty, I thought about Paulina and laid a pillow sideways to fill the space she'd normally take up.

It happened in the middle of the night. The voices awoke me. Tía Amelia's tirade. I followed my father downstairs. The living room was dark, my mother and Gonzalo at the far end, my aunt on the stairs.

"What's going on?" papá asked.

"I found them right there."

Tía sounded like her mouth was full of stones.

"I came downstairs for a glass of water," Gonzalo explained.

"And I," said my mother, "was reading because I couldn't sleep."

"Reading with no light?" tía Amelia wanted to know.

It wasn't raining. Outside, the world was like a sleeping giant, the sound of the sea its breath. Inside was all shadows, our silhouettes and the furniture blacker than the darkness.

"The lamp went out. Gonzalo was helping me light it."

"Do you think I'm an idiot, Claudia?"

"You're drunk," my mother said.

"And you're a two-faced sneak," said my aunt, unable to stand up straight.

"Oh for God's sake. Did it look like we were up to anything?"

My aunt, unable to speak, stared at my mother.

"I say this with love, Amelia: You're intoxicated,

seeing things that aren't there. I knew it was a bad idea to come on vacation with you."

My mother walked straight past her and took my father by the arm.

"Let's go."

We walked upstairs and into our bedroom and went to bed. Only the sea's calm breath remained.

First thing in the morning we packed up. Already bathed and dressed, we went downstairs with our suitcases. Tía Amelia and Gonzalo were having breakfast at the dining room table. We left without saying goodbye. Without even looking at them.

That was the last time we were together.

"DO YOU AND your mother ever stop by at Zas?"

My father asked me this the day after we got back from La Bocana. Or the day after that. Whichever day, it was while we were out, just the two of us, without mamá. It had rained that night and the morning was milky, everything covered in a film of white. I looked at my father, thinking, why are you doing this to me? He, armed with a smile, wanted an answer. I sighed.

"Yes."

"Do you go inside?"

"Sometimes."

"And sometimes you stay outside and Gonzalo comes out?"

The smile frozen on his face.

"Yes."

"And on Wednesdays, when she takes you to art class, does mamá go in with you or does she leave?"

"She leaves."

"And does she take a long time to come pick you up?"

I hated him.

"Can we talk about something else?"

His smile melted. He grabbed my hand and we continued walking down the riverside avenue. The city, gloomy and desolate, like the inside of a very old house.

The following Wednesday my mother stopped the Renault 12 outside the academy. She waited for me to get out and go in. The sky was steamy. The street was littered with sticks and fallen leaves—brown, yellow, green—that humidity had plastered to the pavement. It felt cool and slimy and we were both in long sleeves.

From the door to the academy I turned to her. I could have told her not to go. We're going to learn how to do portraits today, please stay. Even though I had a photo of her to copy, having mamá as a model would be better. You're pretty in the photo, but prettier in real life. She was wearing a yellow high-necked blouse, red lipstick, and had her hair up in an elegant ponytail. They know. She waved goodbye. Don't go today, I could have said.

Mamá pulled away.

Class ended and I went outside to wait for her. Sometimes she was early and sometimes it took half an hour. I don't remember her being later than usual that day.

I sat on the wall under the eaves of the old house. It was drizzling just lightly. Students walked in and out of the academy, passing by. The mosaic tiles on the ground were faded. I got up. Started jumping from tile to tile, imagining a hopscotch. I got hot. Took off my sweatshirt, tied it around my waist, and kept hopping.

The Renault 12 pulled up. Mamá, radiant, her shirt collar up, ponytail intact, lipstick perfect. I sat beside her.

"You're all sweaty," she said.

"Turn sideways."

"What for?"

"I can't get your nose right."

"Are you painting me?"

"Drawing, for now."

She obeyed.

"I see now," I said. "It's a triangle."

"My nose?"

"I was doing it round."

"I want to see this drawing when you're finished."

"It's going to be an oil painting. In ochre colors."

"With a mustard-yellow background. Mustard yellow favors me."

"Okay, namesake," I said. "I'll do it the same color as our car."

We arrived at the supermarket. She took a basket. We said hi to Doña Imelda on the way in, and she followed us with her eyes in a way I understood only later. My mother walked down the right aisle, the milk and eggs aisle, and I started down the middle one.

I stopped for a minute at the candy rack, trying to decide what I wanted. Hard candy or soft, sweet or sour, colored or white. I selected a red Bon Bon Bum.

Then I went to my father's office. To my surprise tía Amelia was there. Sitting at papá's desk, which was huge and metal and made her look small, though scary as a queen. Her eyebrows were drawn on, her makeup dark, and she wore a black shirt with big shoulder pads.

"Where's my father?"

"Hello, sweetie," she said with a smile that vanished the moment she saw my mother.

Mamá shifted the basket to her other arm.

"What are you doing here, Amelia?"

"My baby brother might be a bit dopey but he's on to you now."

"What are you talking about?"

"He knows about the two of you."

"Oh, please, are you really going to carry on with all that? Have you been drinking?"

My aunt, calm as you please, said, "He saw you with him today, Claudia."

My mother froze.

"Watched you pick him up, saw where you went."

Mamá grabbed my hand.

"Let's go, your tía is getting crazier by the day."

We sped down the aisle. Stopped at the register. Mamá dropped my hand to deal with the groceries.

"Such a pretty color on you," said Doña Imelda, meaning the yellow of her blouse.

It was clear something was wrong—my father had gone out, tía Amelia was sitting in for him in the office, my mother was all flustered—but Doña Imelda acted like everything was the same as ever.

"What a winter, mmm? Just won't stop raining."

She gazed out at the gray sheets lashing down over the world. Mamá said something or other and pulled out her wallet. Her hands trembled. Doña Imelda noticed and didn't say another word.

We got back in the car. Drove home in silence, as if on our way to a funeral. Except that our silence wasn't sad but electric. I didn't even dare to unwrap my Bon Bon Bum.

My mother went straight to her nightstand and picked up the phone. I stood at my bedroom door, where she couldn't see me but I could hear her. First she spoke in hushed tones. Soon she became distraught and raised her voice.

"He was supposed to be on until closing. ... He didn't say anything? ... If he comes in, if you see him, if he phones, please tell him to call me."

She was tense the rest of the afternoon. Pacing her bedroom and the hallway, always close to the phone—which never rang—unable to lie down and read her magazines or to sit still. I pretended to watch TV in the study.

It got dark, and still papá didn't come home. We ate dinner. My mother in silence, and me, like Doña Imelda, pretending nothing was wrong, chattering about one thing and another. Art class, my portrait, jokes María del Carmen told at school, the jungle and how sinister it looked that night.

"Don't you think? Like something out of a scary movie."

Outside: soft tireless rain, and Cali River growing ever louder.

We finished dinner. Like usual, we watched TV and then at eight o'clock she sent me off to brush my teeth and go to bed.

My pillow was all damp and cold, and something hard, like a ball of glass, was stuck in my chest. Lulled by the whisper of drizzle and the hollow sound of droplets hitting the pavement, I drifted slowly off to sleep.

At some point, without my realizing it, the drizzle

turned into a storm, and the storm filtered into my dream. Lightning flashed, everything lit up and the boom woke me.

My room was still and outside it had stopped raining altogether.

The storm was in my parents' room. The storm was my father's voice. A voice rising from within, not from his mouth but his belly, like the way the ground rumbles before an earthquake. My mother's voice, a thin strand, audible in his pauses. I couldn't make out what they were saying. Only the shouting and vibration. Only the fury. She raised her voice and, for once, I heard her clearly:

"Then we'll separate!"

And papá: "I'll leave you out on the street, you and him both!"

My bedroom door was ajar. There was a little light in the hall. I got up and crept slowly. They kept shouting. I went into the hall. Their bedroom door was open slightly and I could see my father. Skinny, hunched, shirt wrinkled, bald spot shining in the light, his few white hairs disheveled. The words he shouted flew from his mouth like darts, deformed by rage. He grabbed my mother, tousled and in her pajamas, by the arm, shook her and pushed her onto the bed.

I took a step. They sensed me and turned. My mother on the bed, my father's eyes like stones. He strode to the door and slammed it shut. The shouting stopped. Now there was no sound. Only silence. Only the abyss that was their silence.

I returned to my bedroom crying, grabbed Paulina and curled up with her in the corner of the bed.

PART TWO

MY PARENTS DID not separate the following morning. The three of us had breakfast together like we did every day, me all ready for school and them in pajamas, silent.

"Lucila," I said once we'd left the house, "last night my parents had a horrible fight."

"Watch where you step," she said pointing to a squishy lump of fresh dog doo.

"They're going to separate."

She didn't say anything.

"Did you hear me?"

"Yes, but I'm going to act like I didn't."

"Why?"

"Because that's not for you to talk about, Miss Claudia. That's your parents' business."

Lucila was hardly taller than me, though as broad and square as an elevator. She wore a blue housecoat with no apron and her hair—black, starting to gray—in two braids wrapped around her head. Between her eyebrows was the vertical wrinkle of a grouch, a deep up-and-down line.

When we got to school she handed me my lunchbox and we said goodbye. That afternoon, like always, she was waiting for me when I got out.

"Miss Claudia," she said.

"Is my mother home?"

"Yes."

"What about my father?"

"He had lunch and went back to the supermarket."

We walked home in silence, me hearing my father shouting, replaying the fight in my head. *I'll put you out on the street, you and him both.*

Back at the apartment, everything was the same. The jungle and its plants. The furniture in its place. My mother in bed with a magazine. My father's things on the nightstand. Both of their clothes in the closet. Jars and bottles in the bathroom. Nothing unusual happened that afternoon. My father came home at the normal time and that night the three of us had dinner just like always. They watched the news, and at eight o'clock I went to bed.

The following day, the same thing. My parents pretending nothing was wrong, even though he was sleeping in the study. I noticed when I got up to go to the bathroom and saw him through the half-open door, arranging pillows on the sofa. A bald little man with a hook-shaped body.

Before, the routine was different on Saturdays. We'd get up later, take turns bathing, and have breakfast after we got dressed, mamá in her red gym bodysuit. She would drop us off at the supermarket and then go on to her aerobics class.

That Saturday my mother woke me up as usual. I took a bath after my father, got dressed and brushed my hair in my bedroom, and then went down for breakfast. He was dressed, she was in pajamas.

"Aren't you going to the gym?" I asked.

It was him who responded: "No."

I'll put you on the street.

I looked at mamá.

"No," she echoed, "but you're going to the supermarket."

They were like robots. Not looking at each other, not talking to each other.

I looked at papá.

"That's right," he said, "you're coming with me."

I turned to her.

"What are you going to do?"

"Nothing."

Then we'll separate, she'd said.

"You're not going out?"

"Where would I go, Claudia?"

"But then why do I have to go to the supermarket?"

"Because it's good for you to get out."

"Learn how it runs," he added.

So maybe they weren't going to separate and things would carry on as usual. Without Gonzalo. *I'll put you out on the street, you and him both.* I pictured *him* in my head. Dirty, bearded, his clothes in tatters, muscles wasted away, hair frizzy and thin like it was at La Bocana when he came out of the ocean. A beggar, lost, someplace far from the city.

Doña Imelda appointed me bagger at the checkout. She rang up people's items and I sorted them and put them into different bags based on whether they were groceries, refrigerated, fragile, or soft.

In the building across the street lived a little old lady who did her shopping at the supermarket. She was frail and hunchbacked, had hair that was dyed orange, and wore clothes that were too big, like they belonged to someone else. Doña Imelda had known her forever, they began chatting.

"Remember when her mother used to carry her around in a little basket?" the old lady said. *Her* meaning me.

"Perky little thing, she was."

"With those big wide eyes."

"Held her head up all by herself."

"And started speaking so quick."

"Not even a year and half old and she was talking up a storm. I remember when she was about five. Sounded just like a grown-up, using all those big words."

"Well, sure, with no brothers or sisters, raised surrounded by adults ..."

The old lady and Doña Imelda looked at me.

"And now look at her ..."

Which they did, head to toe.

"Such an intelligent girl."

"So clever."

They were only insisting on my intelligence, I realized, because they couldn't say I was pretty.

"Shame her grandfather never got to meet her," the old lady said.

Doña Imelda nodded, then thought better.

"Or maybe not, you know?"

"Oh, she'd have changed him, no doubt. Grandchildren do that."

"They do, yes," Doña Imelda agreed.

I handed the old lady the bag of spaghetti, butter, and tomatoes she'd bought. She patted my head goodbye and began walking, slow and careful, one little step after the next, looking like it would take her an eternity to get to the other side of the street. When she was finally a good ways off, I turned to Doña Imelda.

"Why is it better my grandfather didn't meet me?"

She looked around to be sure there was nobody around.

"He was a difficult man."

"Difficult how?"

"Full of long silences, like his father, and when he did speak it was only to scold somebody."

In his wedding portrait my grandfather wasn't smiling. Still, I thought, that unattractive man must have felt so lucky to have a bride so young and beautiful. And must have been devastated when he lost her. Which was why he hadn't raised children. Why he didn't visit them or buy them shoes. The poor man couldn't take the pain of staying on the farm where he'd lived with her.

We had very few photos of my father's family. They were old and black-and-white. Loose, stuck in between the pages of mamá's photo albums. The coffee farm. Tía Amelia and papá with their notebooks. The aunt who raised them, a square woman with black curls and a mean face. My grandfather in a broadcloth suit. My grandfather with his children when they came to the city, two narrow-hipped kids, looking like survivors from a war. The supermarket on the day of its grand opening. An old car. Tía Amelia and papá at their school graduation. My grandfather on the balcony at his house, a tube up his nose. In none of them was he smiling. He had a furrowed brow and a mouth that pulled downward. Clearly an expression of sorrow, I'd thought. Until Doña Imelda came along with her comment.

"Did my grandfather ever scold you?"

"All the time."

"Did he get really mad?"

"Terribly mad." She leaned closer and lowered her voice. "And with your father, he was even worse. What I think is, since your abuelita died in childbirth, he blamed your father. Imagine that, his own son, just a poor little baby with no mama."

My father was in his office, adding things up on a calculator and noting them down in a logbook. The fan, sitting on top of a metal filing cabinet, was rotating slowly and making a racket like it was about to break down. Sensing me at the door, he looked up.

"Was your aunt good to you?" I asked.

The question surprised him.

"Tía Mona?"

I nodded.

"I think so," he said.

"Did you love her like a mother?"

"I don't know."

"Because you never had a mother?"

"I don't know."

He thought about it.

"What I remember most is her smell."

"What did she smell like?"

"Talcum powder."

"Nice?"

"Yes."

"How old were you when she died?"

"Eight."

"Like me."

"Yep."

"Do you remember when you went to live with your father?"

"Yes."

"Did you like it?"

"His house was more modern than the farm."

"But did you like it?"

"My father's house?"

"Moving back in with him?"

"Not so much."

"Because you were used to your tía and the farm?"

"Because he beat me with a cable."

"Your father beat you with a cable?"

"Yes."

"Why?"

"I don't remember."

I gasped. It was like I was seeing him for the first time. He looked at his watch.

"Lunchtime."

He set his pencil on the notebook. Stood. Came over and put a hand on my shoulder.

"Shall we go?"

He smiled. An orphan. A real orphan. Not like mamá who when she was a little girl had felt like one but wasn't.

On Sundays, after breakfast, papá and I would go for a walk.

We'd wander around our neighborhood, or the supermarket neighborhood. Climb up and down hills. Look at old buildings and big houses with stone walls. Walk up to the top of a steep street, to the statue of Sebastián de Belalcázar. We'd be all red and sweaty when we got there, hoping to find somebody with a snowcone or popsicle cart. Then we'd sit on the wall and look down at the city, so flat and wide, and the trees, and the clouds.

Or we'd wander down the avenue by the river, where it was always cooler because of the trees that were so fat we couldn't wrap our arms around them. From the bridges, we'd watch the water, churning dark and thick if it rained, flowing steady and blue-gray the rest of the time. On a flat stretch at the mouth of the Aguacatal River was a tree with a horizontal trunk I liked to climb.

Sometimes we went to the zoo. Other times, we just walked past it and headed out toward the restaurant called Cali Viejo and beyond, where the houses and sidewalks ended and the edges of the path were lined with crunchy, bleached-out vegetation and skinny trees that had gnarled branches.

I would talk. Tell my father what was going on at school. He would listen and laugh when he was supposed to. I'd ask questions about things that were important and trivial, about life, the universe, nature. He would ponder and give me his answer, which was always precise, or say he didn't know and fall silent.

Like people drowned in a calm sea, my father's dead, I began to think, resided in his silences.

ON OUR WALK the Sunday after the fight, I decided to keep my mouth shut, not ask questions, and see how long my father could go in silence. We walked out of the apartment, took the elevator down, headed up the avenue, walked to the zoo, and not a word. I thought for sure he was going to have to speak at the ticket office.

"One adult, one child?" the woman asked.

He nodded, and then smiled his thanks.

We went in and walked across the bridge over the river. The morning sky was white, but the sun and swelter were both rising. It was a relief to take refuge in the bird enclosure, a huge warehouse thing with a mesh dome, stone walls, and plenty of vegetation for shade.

We ambled slowly, looking at the parrots and other brightly colored birds in among the frogs and plants, the dusky-legged guans, the ducks in their little ponds. Not a word from papá. He didn't even point at anything. Just looked. The longer we went, the more stifling the heat, and by the end it felt like there wasn't any air left to breathe.

When we pushed open the doors to leave the enclosure, it was like pulling your head out of water.

Papá wiped the sweat from his face and neck with his handkerchief. There was a giant ceiba tree and we watched the condors from under its shade. Their cage was tall but narrow, and they were all the way at the top, looking down at the world from their thrones like very ugly kings.

Then we continued down the path parallel to the river. There were blue patches in the sky now and the sun pulsed over our heads, but it felt comfortable because the trees provided shade, you could hear the river, there were hardly any people, and the path was wide.

We came to the boa constrictor's cage. It was stock-still on a log, fat and shiny, a long part of its body straight, then coiled, then another part straight again. It looked endless. Suddenly the snake moved, its head pointed at us, and we saw its forked tongue dart out, black and flat as a ribbon. Papá had no reaction. I grabbed his hand, terrified.

We returned to the path, where we came across the giant Galápagos tortoise. His name was Carlitos and, right up till he died, he always roamed free around the zoo. Carlitos lumbered along awkwardly in his big shell, rough as a terracotta pot. I wanted to be his friend and ride on his back. I looked at my father, dying to tell him. He smiled and I found the strength to keep quiet.

The crocodiles were sunbathing in their cloudy-watered lake, dry, cracked, and as still as the dead. My father's and my hands were sweating where we held them, and he showed no sign of being bothered by this or anything else.

We moved on to the rhinoceroses, which looked like they were made of clay, modeled by hand, wrinkled and grooved. Up ahead, some kids screamed that the deer had had babies. I dropped my father's hand and ran.

There were two fawns, all wobbly on their skinny little legs. They reminded me of Bambi, who lost his mother and was all alone in the forest with a father he didn't know, and I was filled with a bottomless sorrow that felt ancient. Papá caught up and stood beside me, but it was like he wasn't there. The silence erased him. The challenge of not speaking was torture, it was stupid, I thought, and yet I did not speak.

When we got to where the zebras were, I focused on them. After staring for a while, their stripes started to blend together and look fake, as if they were painted, like posters to put on the wall.

Straight ahead was the brown bear. We went over and it stretched, got up, and ambled off, hips swinging, to get in the pool.

The spectacled bear never came out.

The lions, up on their boulder, only yawned.

The tiger was asleep in the shade.

For a minute, looking at the anteater, I couldn't tell which end was the head and which was the tail.

The baboons, bored, scratched their heads and armpits.

The New World monkeys, out on their island, leapt from branch to branch, swinging and screeching like mad.

Then we came to the end of the path, and still not a word from papá. Leaving the zoo, we went back down the same avenue in the suffocating midday heat. Me, defeated, and him indifferent, as though the silence had sucked up his soul and rather than a man walking beside me, there was an empty shell.

We took the elevator up to the apartment. Mamá, who was setting the table for lunch—roast chicken, delivered—asked how it had gone. My father assumed I would answer. I pressed my lips together. She repeated the question, and without looking at her, he said:

"Fine."

We sat. The two of them stiff as boards, addressing only me.

That night, to keep from feeling like I was at a ping-pong match, I brought Paulina down and put her in the chair where no one sat.

The following Sunday, again we headed down the river avenue toward the zoo, but instead of going straight we turned at the old pedestrian bridge, walked across it and wandered around the supermarket neighborhood until, without me so much as opening my mouth, papá said, "That *sun!*"

A giant egg yolk in the middle of the sky.

"Maybe your aunt has a little juice to offer us."

I stared at him in shock.

"Aren't you thirsty?"

I conceded that I was.

"Shall we go see?"

I stared, wondering what mamá would think of this. He smiled.

"Okay," I said.

Tía Amelia came out onto her balcony to see who was ringing the bell and looked surprised to see us. She sent the key down in a little basket on a string.

My aunt waited for us outside the apartment, on the landing, in her knee-length nightie and hugged us both at the same time.

We went in. She poured us pineapple juice, cold from the fridge. We drank it down in one gulp. She poured more and we went and sat in the living room. She asked me how I was, what I was up to, how things were going at school, what I was learning in art class. I said we were working on human faces, I was doing so-so in math, I wasn't up to anything special, María del Carmen had chickenpox, and I was fine.

"What about you?"

"Fine."

I wanted to ask about her Gonzalo. Where he was, what had happened, if she still saw him or whether they spoke. I didn't dare.

"Did you miss me?" she asked.

"Yes."

"I missed you more."

She spread her arms. I went to the wicker chair and sat on her lap and stayed for a while, until she lit a cigarette and it stank. She started asking papá about the supermarket, which I used as an excuse to get up.

There were still two beds in the bedroom. But no magazines by the bathroom. Or dumbbells. While my aunt and father talked, I wandered around the apartment trying to find some sign of Gonzalo. I looked in the bathroom drawers, the kitchen drawers, the shower and the closet, on the nightstands, in the chest of drawers. I went back to the living room. Searched my aunt's face, my father's face, the things they said and the things they didn't. But found nothing.

I wanted to believe that Gonzalo had left of his own accord, taking only what he'd brought and that my father, at most, had made him sign a paper saying he couldn't get anything, like he'd said the night we met him.

Before my parents' fight, before mamá and tía Amelia's fight, before Gonzalo came into the family, there were things I took for certain. Mothers had children because they wanted them. Tía Amelia was happy living in her mini-apartment, with her housedresses. My grandfather was a sad man. My father, the best in the world.

Now, after the fights and Gonzalo, beneath the layers of my burned convictions, at my core which had been clear as an onion, throbbed the fear that my father had done something bad. Something worse than make Gonzalo sign a paper and put him out on the street. Something I'd rather not imagine and that would be best to erase from my mind.

I looked at him and he looked the same as before. A man with a goofy face who appeared incapable of doing harm. But inside, where the orphan was, in that sea of silence, I knew there lived a monster.

We went home. Mamá was on a little bench with a garden fork, working the soil of the aguacatillo. Papá said to the air that he had to go to the bathroom. Mamá, to me, that she'd ordered Cuban sandwiches.

Me: "We went to tía Amelia's today."

My mother went rigid, bent over the dirt. My father kept going up the stairs. Slowly, she turned to me and waved me over with one hand. She waited until my father got to the second floor and went into the bathroom.

"What did she say?" mamá asked quietly.

"Nothing."

"What did you talk about?"

"How we are, what we've been up to and the supermarket."

"Did she say anything about me?"

"No."

"If she ever does, don't believe her. She's a liar."

I stared at her, expressionless.

"Got it?"

"I heard you, yes."

"You can't believe anything your tía Amelia says, Claudia."

MY MOTHER, THOSE days, was still listening for the phone, and when it rang she'd run to pick up. I could hear her excitement as she said hello and her disenchantment on discovering who it was. Gloria Inés, the bank manager, a wrong number.

The mute no longer called and she began to grow increasingly upset. She'd pace the jungle. Sit at her dressing table and then get up a second later. Lie on her bed and do the same. One afternoon she got out her gardening tools, shears, trowel, gardening fork, bucket, gloves, fertilizer, the little bench, all of it, and a minute later, far too soon, I saw her sitting on her bed, facing the wall.

"Is señora finished with her plants?" Lucila asked from the first floor, as shocked as I was.

"Yes."

"Should I put her things away?"

"Please."

"I think the plants need to be watered, Señora Claudia."

"You're right."

"Should I water them?"

"Alright, Lucila, thank you."

My mother grabbed a magazine. Opened it, flicked through two pages and dropped it. Watching from the door, I went in. Sat down on her bed and picked up the magazine. An *¡Hola!*, newly arrived. Lady Di on the cover. I opened it.

"Look at Sophia Loren."

Before the fights and Gonzalo, she would be the one showing me photos of Sophia Loren. She said the two of them had the same skin tone. Now she gave the woman only a passing glance.

"The two of you have the same skin tone."

No response. She bit a fingernail.

In the before times, my mother was obsessed with Natalie Wood, a famous actress who was found dead, floating facedown in the ocean. In her nightgown, my mother said, and wool socks and a red jacket, with her hair fanned out in the water like a jellyfish. For weeks she talked of nothing else.

Natalie Wood's husband, Robert Wagner, was also famous, also an actor. The couple had been out on their yacht with Christopher Walken, yet another famous actor, who she was filming a movie with. The three of them drank, had dinner, and drank some more. It was the dead of night, the sea was rough. Natalie said goodnight and went to bed, leaving the men in the living room. Her husband said that sometime later, when he was going to bed, he realized she wasn't in their cabin, and when he searched the yacht for her he realized the rubber dinghy was gone too and assumed she'd taken it out for a bit, so he waited up, and then after a while got worried and radioed for the authorities.

The authorities found her the next day, according to my mother, and ruled her death accidental.

"Accidental, my ass," mamá said.

No one but the authorities believed the husband's story. Who goes out barefoot, in a nightgown, in the middle of the night, in an inflatable dingy, in dark rough waters? Everybody thought the husband had actually found her in the cabin and, jealous of Christopher Walken, had a fight with her and threw her overboard. Everybody but mamá.

"If he'd thrown her overboard, she'd have taken off her jacket, she'd have swum or screamed, grabbed onto the yacht or the rubber dinghy ..."

"What, then?"

"She jumped overboard herself."

I couldn't find Natalie Wood in the new ¡Hola! I did, though, find Princess Grace of Monaco, whose car-crash death my mother had also been obsessed with.

News of it was on TV and in the papers, but they only gave the basics. And the magazines that would have had more substantial stories and photos took weeks to get from Europe to the Librería Nacional.

Tía Amelia was there at the time, married to Gonzalo, unbeknownst to us. She phoned from Madrid to say everything was fine. My father and I stood beside mamá while she spoke, very fast since long-distance calls were so expensive back then, and very loud, as though to ensure her voice carried across the ocean. Before hanging up, my mother asked her to send every magazine she could get her hands on about Princess Grace's death.

They arrived quickly that way, and my mother set about reading them all. One afternoon, while I was doing my homework, she walked into the study with a magazine held open in one hand.

"Listen to this," she said, reading a few lines which explained that one part of the road had a very sharp curve where drivers had to use their brakes and steer carefully. Then she looked up: "The princess didn't."

"That's awful."

"She kept driving straight, plowed the retaining wall right down. Can you imagine?"

"Terrible."

"She was tired of all her obligations."

"What?"

"She picked the most dangerous route and didn't even brake on that curve."

"You think she didn't brake on purpose?"

"She hated driving and had chauffeurs, but that day, despite having a headache, she insisted on doing it herself."

"And drove off the cliff on purpose?"

I'd seen the photos in those magazines, her upside-down car in the ravine.

"Without caring about her family?"

Photos of her funeral. The pain on her husband's and children's faces. Photos of Stephanie, the youngest child, who was in the car with her and had to wear a neck brace for a while.

"Or what would happen to Stephanie?"

"She was tired of her obligations," mamá repeated.

The photo I found of Princess Grace of Monaco was a small black-and-white one that showed her in the coffin. The article talked about New Year's parties in Monaco, and how there would be no celebrations that year because of the mourning. The princess, laid out on elegant white fabric in her casket, had shiny hair, her hands folded over a rosary, eyes closed, and a tranquil expression on her face. She looked younger. Sleeping beauty.

"She's resting now," I told my mother.

"Who is?"

"Princess Grace."

I showed my mother, and, sparked by curiosity, she scrutinized her.

"Yes."

"She was so tired, wasn't she?"

"Mmm?"

"Of all her obligations."

"Oh, yes," she said, and lay back on the bed, turning her back.

The following day when I got home from school, I found her in her pajamas, lying in bed with a box of tissues, her head on a mound of pillows. Her eyes were red, her nose stuffed, her voice froggy.

"Have you been crying?"

"It's rhinitis."

"What's that?"

"An allergy. I haven't gotten it for a long time."

She grabbed a pack of pills from her nightstand, put one on her tongue and swallowed it down with water.

"The allergy medicine makes me tired. I'm going to sleep for a bit."

And just like the day before, she lay down and turned her back.

Mamá began staying in bed from morning to night. All day long in her pajamas, not even bathing or grooming. A box of tissues by her side. Her nose and eyes red. The curtains drawn. Sometimes not even with a magazine, not even reading, not doing anything at all, just curled in a ball like a cat.

When I got back from school, the first thing I did was go up to her room.

"Hi, namesake."

"Hello."

"How are you?"

"I'm here."

"Are you still sick?"

"A little."

"Is there anything I can bring you?"

"No."

"Should I open the curtains?"

"The light bothers me, Claudia. How many times do I have to tell you?"

"Want to hear what we did today?"

"Later, maybe. I took my allergy medicine and I'm sleepy."

I ate lunch and she slept. I did my homework and she slept. At four o'clock I turned on the television and, as I watched *Sesame Street*, she slept.

Mamá would get out of bed in the late afternoon. Open the curtains. Take a long bath. Put on different pajamas and brush her hair at the dressing table, slowly and mechanically, transfixed at the mirror.

Lucila would bring her up a coffee and some toast and she'd eat in bed. I would sit beside her. Sometimes I could get her to talk, listen to my stories about school, tell me about the women in her magazines or a story about my grandparents. One afternoon she told me that the last time she'd had rhinitis before this was when my grandmother died, and the time before, when my grandfather did.

"What about before that?"

"When I almost didn't pass my second-to-last year of high school."

Other times I couldn't get her to say anything, but I stayed until she finished her coffee and toast anyway.

When my father got home, she'd take another allergy pill, close the curtains, and go back to bed. They no longer hid the fact that they were sleeping apart.

Lucila started doing some of the things Mamá used to do. Making the shopping list, taking care of the plants, getting my uniform ready for the next day. Papá did the rest.

My mother's birthday fell on a Wednesday. That morning, I brought her breakfast up on a tray that Lucila had prepared and told her to be ready for a surprise that afternoon. She smiled. After school, I clarified that when I said that afternoon I meant after art class. She smiled.

I had lunch, and my father came to take me to the academy. When I got back I ran up the stairs.

"Your surprise!"

The room was dark, my mother a lump in the bed.

"What is it?" she said in a leaden voice, like a chain she was forced to drag around.

I pulled her surprise out from behind my back.

"Ta-da!"

The finished portrait. The one I'd copied from a photo. My mother in ochre tones, with the mustard-yellow background she'd requested. Her nose, after many attempts, sophisticated.

"You have to look."

Finally she moved. Sat up. At that point she was in the worst days of her rhinitis. Only getting out of bed to go to the bathroom. She refused the coffee and toast Lucila brought up. Claudia, not now, she'd say when I came in to say hello; Claudia, shut the door; Claudia, leave me alone. So I wasn't expecting her to get out of bed and look at the portrait, tell me how beautiful it was, how well it had turned out, kiss me, or say thank you, let's put it on the wall in the study with the family portraits. But I was expecting her to smile, like she had that morning and when I got home from school, to inspect it, show some kind of approval, a little shine in her eyes, something.

"Claudia, I just took my allergy medicine, I'm sleepy. Can you show me later?"

I lowered the portrait. Then I went to my room and slid it under my bed, with the broken toys and the ones I no longer played with. I grabbed Paulina and set to brushing her long chocolate-colored hair with the tiny Barbie brush.

A few days later when I got back from school, I was shocked to see her room all bright, curtains open, the clock radio on papá's nightstand tuned to the news, and her sitting on the bed.

"Karen Carpenter died this morning," she said.

She was in her pajamas and hadn't bathed or brushed her hair, but looked almost perky, all things considered.

"How?"

"They found her in the closet, naked, though she'd

covered herself with the pajamas she had just taken off to get dressed. Even in death, she behaved like a decent señorita."

Karen Carpenter was the singer and drummer of the brother-sister duo The Carpenters. They dressed like wholesome kids and played catchy, clean-cut soft rock.

"What did she die of?"

"Anorexia."

At that time not much was known about the disease. I'd never even heard of it.

"What's that?"

"It's when people kill themselves by starvation."

The first magazine detailing the story of Karen Carpenter's death arrived a few weeks later. I waited until my mother put it down and then took it to my room. I'd never read a whole article before.

Anorexia nervosa, the article began, was the disease of successful, obedient young women who became obsessed with their weight. They stopped eating, vomited, took laxatives, exercised ceaselessly. These women distrusted the scales if they showed their weight as abnormally low, and even though they were super-skinny, looking in the mirror they saw fat people. They starved themselves for years, became malnourished, and one day their hearts gave out.

One of the photos showed the bones of Karen Carpenter's face jutting out. Her jaw, cheekbones, the arch of her brow, all protruding. Her eyes, round and dark, looked hollow. Almost a skeleton.

She collapsed at her parents' house. So weak the

paramedics couldn't revive her. Thirty-two years old. Pretty, rich, famous, loved by her family and fans. A rock star who personified the best of young people those days. There was no trace of drugs or alcohol in her system. She didn't even smoke. The strongest thing she put in her body was iced tea. Karen Carpenter didn't partake in the excesses of other musicians who'd overdosed. The article listed examples: Jimi Hendrix, Janis Joplin, Elvis Presley. But in her own way she sought the same thing they had, and that was how it ended: in self-destruction.

"What's an overdose?"

Mamá had just taken a bath and was at her dressing table, detangling her long hair with a wide-tooth comb. Behind her in the reflection, a blackberry juice stain on my white uniform top; I looked overheated. Her, fresh; me, sweaty, like we lived in different countries.

"Did you read the article?"

"Yes."

She turned around to tell me.

"It's when someone takes too many drugs."

"And they die?"

"Sometimes."

"By accident?"

"Or on purpose."

"Why would someone do that on purpose?"

She turned back to the mirror and kept combing.

"Ay, Claudia, just because. Because some people don't want to live."

I'd heard of suicide before and thought I knew what it meant but was only now beginning to comprehend. It wasn't that suddenly the person collapsed in a fit of insanity and killed themselves. It wasn't that something happened despite their desires or intentions. It wasn't a game or a prank gone wrong. It was that the person actually wanted to die.

I looked at my mother sitting there—skinny, wan, her nose sore from so much blowing, chest and eyes sunken. I truly saw her.

"Mamá, do you want to live?"

She glanced at me for a second in the reflection. A moment later she looked away.

"Don't be silly."

"Papá, are there people who don't want to live?"

It was Sunday and Cali was deserted. All for us.

"People who don't want to live?"

"Mamá said."

"She told you there were people who didn't want to live?"

"Like Karen Carpenter, she killed herself by starvation."

We were standing at the mouth of the Aguacatal River.

"Your mother told you that?"

"Yes."

"The Carpenter woman had a disease."

The waters of the Cali flowed gently between the rocks.

"Well Princess Grace of Monaco drove off a cliff."

"That was an accident."

"How do you know?"

"They said it on the news."

"What about Natalie Wood?"

"Also an accident."

"They said it on the news?"

"Yes."

The smaller Aguacatal joined the Cali River timidly, as though attempting not to make a fuss.

"Have you ever wanted to kill yourself?" I asked.

"No."

My father, whose gaze was fixed straight ahead, at the stone wall of the old house between the rivers, turned and looked at me.

"You?"

"Me either."

He smiled.

"What about mamá?" I asked, my voice as small as the Aguacatal.

"Of course not," he assured me. "I don't know anyone who wants to kill themselves."

I smiled too, and ran off to climb the tree with the horizontal trunk.

Then Gloria Inés killed herself.

MY MOTHER SAID Gloria Inés was the closest thing she had to a sister. There were no photos of her on the wall in the study but there was one on the little bonsai table, in a wrought silver frame. Black and white. Of the two of them, at the club, by the rain tree. My mother a scrawny girl with long dark hair, masses of it. Hair for a body that deserved it. Gloria Inés wore hers all frizzy, with black cat-eye glasses and a miniskirt that showed off her long, foal thighs. She was much taller than my mother, and curvy, already a woman.

At the time, my mother told me, she was eleven and Gloria Inés was sixteen. And wild. She smoked, put makeup on in the bathroom, went out with boys and had two boyfriends at the same time. The accident occurred about the same time that photo was taken.

Two twins from the club, very popular boys, snuck their parents' car out without permission, and Gloria Inés and her friend drove off with them. They tore down Quinta, sped up, and ran a stop sign—bam, right into a moving truck. The twins barely got a scratch, the friend broke one vertebra and two ribs, and Gloria Inés ended up with her scar. A fat line that ran diagonally down her forehead and split her eyebrow in two.

I didn't think of her as my tía. We rarely saw her, a couple of times a year at most. In addition to being tall, Gloria Inés wore high heels and looked down on people. Her voice was all husky, like a longtime smoker. She wore foundation, eyeshadow, and lipstick, painted on her eyebrows, and had hair even frizzier than it was when she was young. She had two children. Gangly, unattractive teenage boys. Her husband was the shortest person in the whole family, a man with slicked-back hair and a mustache, both jet black.

When we went to their house, the boys would come out in Bermuda shorts, their hair all messy and their legs white, as if they never went to the club. They'd give my mother and me a kiss, shake my father's hand, and go back to their rooms without saying a word. The husband talked about the weather and the news. My father would nod along. My mother would make some offhanded remark in reply. Gloria Inés would raise her split eyebrow.

Their apartment overlooked Avenida de Las Américas from the eighteenth floor. A high wall surrounded the balcony and I had to stand on tiptoe to see out over it. The city, so far below, looked fake: a model with teeny-tiny trees, cars, and people. That void, though, the void felt real. Eighteen stories: a deadly precipice. Not like our apartment stairs, which only felt like one. Looking down, I got a luscious feeling in my tummy and at the same time, since I imagined falling, felt scared to death.

Their apartment floor had brown and gray dots. A desert for Gloria Inés's plants. She had cacti, agave, and succulents, stationed like soldiers, stiff and spaced out in ceramic pots, some with needles, as if wary of people.

Though they had very different taste, my mother and Gloria Inés admired each other's plants. When she came to our apartment, Gloria Inés would sit in the armchair, facing the forest where the tallest ones were.

"You pruned your rubber plants," she might say.

"They were so overgrown," mamá would reply, "we were on the verge of having to move out."

And then my mother at Gloria Inés's house:

"You didn't used to have those donkey tails hanging, did you?"

Donkey tails were the light green plants spilling down like clusters of grapes from the balcony ceiling.

"Poor things were creeping across the floor, long as snakes. I was afraid people would step on them."

They admired one another's plants, and competed.

The last time we saw Gloria Inés was at our apartment, back when my mother was still going to the gym on Saturdays and the mute would hang up if it wasn't her who answered the phone.

As Gloria Inés contemplated the jungle, her husband and children sat on the three-seater sofa. Her husband no doubt brought up the weather or the news. My father nodded, my mother made some blasé comment, and the boys, surrounded by palms, yawned until one of them jumped, startled by their touch. Gloria Inés raised her split eyebrow.

"Do you talk to them, play them music?"

"The plants?" My mother gave a derisive little laugh. "Of course not."

Despite all she did—polish their leaves one by one,

crouch to weed and work the soil—mamá's caretaking was cold, like polishing brass to make it shine.

"They say plants like that very much," Gloria Inés replied defensively. "Mine look so beautiful."

Mamá looked out at her fecund, vibrant jungle and I understood that she was saying: What, and mine don't?

The last time we heard from Gloria Inés was the day of my first communion, after the fights and the death of Karen Carpenter.

Preparing for it kept me very busy. Catechism class with the elementary school principal. Learning the endless new credo, the prayers and mass responses, the songs. Going—with my father, since mamá was still sick with her rhinitis—to dress fittings. Remembering to tell her we had to go to mass on Sundays. Behaving on every occasion.

Confession was two days before, in the school chapel, which was down a long hall. At the back, between heavy red curtains, hung Christ. All skinny and wounded, with nails in him, and his thorny crown and bowed head. A terrifying vision. The tomb of the school's founder was underneath the floor. It was scary in there. The silence above all.

I knelt in the confessional and told the father—a shadow behind the mesh curtain—my sins. That I used to not go to mass hardly ever. That I still didn't make it every week. That I'd looked at naked ladies in *Playboy*. That I had bad thoughts.

"What thoughts?"

"That my tía's husband smells bad and lives on the street. That deep down my father is a bad person.

That mamá doesn't have rhinitis, she's just lazy. That my parents are going to separate ..."

"Anything else?"

"That my mother is going to kill herself. But that one not so much anymore since papá told me it wasn't true."

"Is that all?"

"Yes."

He gave me one Our Father and one Ave María as penance. I stood up. As I was walking off, before the next girl came in to confess, I heard him fidgeting in the confessional.

The night before, while my mother was having her coffee and toast, I told her—because it was true—that the priest had said it was very important for every member of the family to be with us at the ceremony. We were sitting on her bed. Both of us with our legs crossed. Mamá with the tray in front of her.

"I'm going to be there, Claudia."

In the morning mamá got up before us. She bathed and, for the first time since the fight with my father, put on makeup and going-out clothes. A black dress, brown lipstick, and her hair in a ponytail. She didn't exactly look happy but it was almost like she didn't have rhinitis.

My father wore a jacket and tie. Me, my white dress with puffy sleeves and ribbons. She tied my bow in the back and attached my veil. This was the first time since her rhinitis that my mother had done anything like that for me. She handed me a small blue velvet box. Inside was a gold chain with a little angel charm.

"Your grandmother gave that to me the day of my first communion. It's yours now."

She put it on me and we hugged.

The chapel was filled with white flowers. The side doors that overlooked the schoolyard had been opened and morning light streamed in. It was no longer scary. All the girls stood in two lines, each of us holding a candle, which the principal came and lit. As we walked to the altar, singing *A paso lento va la caravana por el sendero del alto peñón / Slowly goes the caravan along the path of the high rock*, I saw tía Amelia in one of the back pews. She was wearing a bright blouse and red lipstick, and when she saw me, she smiled.

My parents were nowhere near her, sitting in one of the front pews, side by side but looking in different directions, my mother at the altar and my father at us girls, smiling his same old smile. We were all dressed the same and I don't think he could tell me from my classmates.

I tried to pay attention during every part of the mass. It was too long, and I spaced out. The priest, who was young and handsome and normally made us all giggly, was now so serious and boring that I had no desire to laugh.

The moment arrived. We stood in order and walked to the altar in pairs. I'd thought that after receiving the host and wine, the body and blood of Christ, I would feel a profound change. That once free of sin and wedded to Him, I would feel light, ready to fly. I concentrated. It was disappointing. The only thing that happened was the host got stuck to the roof of my mouth and I walked back to the pew trying to dislodge it with my tongue, though I pretended to my classmates, and to María del Carmen, who had tears in her eyes, that it had been amazing.

When the ceremony was over, we joined our families in the garden. Mine was the only one not taking pictures. My mother bent over, congratulated me, gave me a kiss, got up, and began to walk home. My father and tía Amelia, who were waiting off to the side, came over. The three of us went to a restaurant for lunch. Then they took me to María del Carmen's party at the club and I forgot about the fights, about Gonzalo, about mamá and her rhinitis, and had fun with my friends.

When I got home my mother sat up in bed. She helped me take off my dress. As I was putting on my pajamas, she folded the dress and stuck it in a bag to take to the launderette. Then she went into her room and came back with another little box, gift wrapped.

"This is from Gloria Inés."

"She was there?"

"She's sick but she sent it with her husband."

I opened it. It was a bracelet with my name written in cursive.

"I love it."

"Tomorrow you'll call and thank her."

The next day was Palm Sunday. I assume I did call her, but I don't remember the conversation, if there was one.

My father worked from Monday to Wednesday. Lucila went to her hometown on vacation so it was just the three of us for Holy Week. Endless days of sun, and movies about the Passion of Christ. My father in his study. My mother in bed in the dark. The jungle twitching on the first floor. The stairs an abyss that suddenly seemed greater than the eighteen stories of Gloria Inés's apartment. Me always with Paulina to keep from feeling so alone at the table, in the study, in my mother's room, in mine.

I was back at school, in Spanish class, with my favorite teacher, when someone knocked on the door. The teacher opened it. She spoke to somebody impossible to see from where I was sitting then turned and looked at the room. At me.

"Claudia, someone's come for you."

"Why?"

You could tell by her face it was serious.

"Get your things."

"What's wrong?"

All the other girls were staring at me from their desks. The teacher didn't say anything. She came over, helped me gather my notebooks and school supplies. She put her arm around me and walked me to the door. Feeling weak in the legs, I didn't dare imagine anything. María del Carmen brought over my lunchbox, which I'd forgotten, and handed it to me.

Lucila, short and squat, was outside the room, braids clipped to her head, the deep wrinkle between her brows furrowed like a scar. My teacher closed the door. Lucila and I stood there in the hallway, which was emptier than I'd ever seen it. Fearing the answer, I couldn't ask a single question.

"Señora Gloria Inés died."

The first thing I felt was relief that it wasn't my mother. The second, I think, was guilt at the relief. The third, that it couldn't be true.

"That's not true," I said.

Lucila, abrupt as ever, looked at me.

"I'm sorry."

"It's true?"

"Yes."

"What happened?"

"I don't know, Miss Claudia. Let's go, your mother's waiting for you at home."

She took my lunchbox and we walked down the hall. The huge old school, the high ceilings, the gigantic floor tiles, and a silence that would have been total were it not for the plasticky sound of our footsteps.

My mother was standing at the top of the staircase. She looked like a crazy lady. Sobbing, barefoot, in white pajamas, her disheveled hair hiding her face. A crazy or a ghost. La Llorona. I dropped my schoolbag and walked up the stairs.

"I just can't believe it," she said.

I put my arm around her waist and she let me guide her to her room. We sat on the edge of her bed.

"How did she die?"

"She killed herself."

"What do you mean?"

"She committed suicide."

"How?"

"Jumped off the balcony."

"All the way to the street?"

"Eighteen stories."

I imagined the fall. Gloria Inés, somersaulting through the air. Head up, head down. Just like Princess Grace of Monaco when her car flew off the cliff. Gloria Inés, smashed into the sidewalk. Long and voluptuous. Her curly hair fanned out on the pavement. Natalie Wood on asphalt.

"Her husband said she was up on a bench watering the hanging plants. The donkey tails, remember?"

"Yes."

"And she fell."

My hand was still on her back. I stroked it. She'd gotten so skinny she was like a stick figure. Karen Carpenter.

"So it was an accident."

"Of course not. The donkey tails were on the inside of the balcony, not out at the edge, and nobody falls over a balcony wall. I don't even believe she was watering the plants."

"Then why would her husband say that?"

"He can't say she jumped."

"Why not?"

"So she can be buried in the cemetery."

"What do you mean?"

"People who commit suicide can't have a catholic burial, it's forbidden."

I could not fathom this.

"But why?"

"Suicide is a mortal sin."

In catechism class, I'd learned that if a person died in mortal sin, without confessing or repenting, they couldn't go to heaven.

"Is Gloria Inés going to hell?"

This triggered my mother's wailing.

"Well," I said. "Maybe she repented."

"Plus, he must be ashamed," she said, once she'd calmed down. "Gloria Inés had depression."

Mamá bathed, dressed in black, and put her hair up in a bun. She was just starting to do her makeup at the vanity when my father came home. He went straight to her. He bent down. My mother, who'd been facing the mirror, turned. For the first time since the fight, they were up close. They looked at one another. She cried, and he put his hand on hers.

"Everything's going to be okay, mija."

My parents dropped me off at tía Amelia's and went to the wake. My aunt asked if I was sad. On a whim I told the truth, that I wasn't. Immediately I felt bad. Gloria Inés was the last remaining relative on my mother's side.

"It's just that we barely ever saw her."

"You're under no obligation to feel sad."

"I am shocked, though."

"Me too, and I hardly knew her."

"Is she going to hell?"

"Why would you think that?"

"Because she committed suicide ..."

"Your mother told you that?"

I nodded yes.

"Well, that's what your mother thinks."

"It's not true?"

She made a who-knows face.

"Gloria Inés is the only one with the truth."

My aunt helped me with my homework. We played dominoes and ate sausages with oven fries and ketchup. She poured herself a glass of wine and I put on my pajamas and brushed my teeth with my finger because I forgot to pack my toothbrush. She finished her glass of wine, thankfully didn't pour another, and smoked her last cigarette on the balcony. Leaning on the railing, the two of us looked out at the night, which was clear, like it was almost dawn, like everybody was asleep. We went into her room to lay down. Her in her bed. Me and Paulina in Gonzalo's. The breeze coming in through the open balcony door blew the gauzy curtains, puffing them out and then sucking them back in, over and over.

"Tía, do you feel lonely?"

Outside, the city was still paused.

"Sometimes."

"Paulina is my favorite doll."

"I know."

"She does everything with me. Has dinner with my parents, watches TV, goes to sleep. Over Semana Santa we spent every second together. Thank you for giving her to me."

"It was my great pleasure."

Light from the street was shining into the room, reflecting me and my tía in the vanity mirror. Two itty-bitty bodies in two matching beds. Behind us, at the vanishing point, like in art class drawings with perspective, the darkness was never-ending.

"Do you feel lonely, sweetheart?"

"Sometimes."

Then some people walked down the street and Cali

came back to life. Footsteps, voices, a barking dog, a car in the distance.

"Want to come sleep with me in my bed?"

"Paulina too?"

"Better if it's just you."

I considered it for a second and made up my mind. But first I got Paulina nice and comfy in her bed. Head on the pillow, eyes closed, sheet pulled up to her neck so she wouldn't get cold. My tía and I arranged ourselves in her bed. We were both on our sides, facing each other. She lay an arm across me. The smell of cigarettes was stuck to her skin, even wafted out from inside her, through her mouth, as if she had a belly full of ash. And with that dirty smell and the weight of her arm, I fell asleep.

I didn't wake up when my parents arrived. In the car, I half woke. Papá lifted me out and carried me in. He put me into bed in my room, in the dark. Then he paused at the door, leaving it open. A stooped shadow. Slowly, he walked into the light of the hallway and down the corridor, not to the study but to my parents' room.

My mother's voice was audible: "She stopped taking her antidepressants."

I sat up in bed and pictured them. Her at the vanity, still dressed, hair up in a bun, a Kleenex in one hand, the tub of makeup remover in the other. Him walking wearily to the clothes rack.

"Her friend told me, the one I introduced you to."

"The short one?"

"Yes, her. She'd spent two months in her bedroom with curtains drawn, watching the same movies on

Betamax. *Love Story* and *Somewhere in Time*. There were so many times I thought it had been too long since we'd spoken, told myself I should call ..."

They fell silent. Her staring into space, at the mirror, I imagined, makeup off, pale now, bags under her eyes, nose red. Him behind her, in the reflection. An exhausted man, shirt untucked, undoing his buttons one by one.

Then her voice again: "But I didn't. And her husband and sons didn't do anything either."

My parents went back to sleeping together, to looking at each other, to talking. She still spent a lot of time in bed, but now she read magazines, bathed, brushed her hair, came downstairs, tended to her plants, and ate with us.

One Sunday, a few weeks after Gloria Inés died, we went out as a family. Our first time since the fight. My father drove, my mother beside him. Me in the middle of the back seat, with Paulina on my lap, blabbering nonstop: it was almost the end of the year, the seven and nine times tables were impossible, I hoped I wasn't going to flunk math or have to take a remedial exam, wouldn't it be so nice for us to all go on vacation, mamá looked so pretty.

"Doesn't she, papá?"

"She does."

One time, one of his old classmates that we bumped into at the amusement park asked if she was his daughter. She looked like his daughter now too. Mamá was wearing blue jeans and a wide-necked black T-shirt that fell off one shoulder, and she had her hair in a girlish high pony.

"Claudia," she said, turning to me, "I know you're excited, but Gloria Inés's husband and children are very sad. You need to calm down."

"Yes, mamá."

Gloria Inés's sons, as ever, emerged from their rooms with messed-up hair, in shorts, greeted us halfheartedly, and went back to their rooms.

"They're wrecks," the husband said.

And my mother: "It's no wonder."

She brought up current events. The husband tried to show some interest but quickly fell silent. Next, mamá talked about the weather. The husband, his hair and mustache perfect, sipped his coffee and the only one to reply was my father.

"Summer's almost here."

Without Gloria Inés, no one had anything to talk about, and that horrible balcony was right outside. The donkey tails, long and pale, hung before the windows, a few steps from the precipice. The cacti, agave, and succulents were still inside, wary as ever.

"Who's taking care of the plants?" asked my father.

Mamá gave him a horrified look and the husband buried his head in his hands.

After a second failed visit, we stopped going back.

A few weeks later, when life was almost back to before the fights and Gonzalo, the apartment door opened from inside just as Lucila stuck her key in the lock. My mother stood there, hair done, all made up, dressed colorfully in bright striped pants, a white sleeveless blouse, and red heels. Seeing her like that, in the middle of the jungle, shocked me even more than finding her crying at the top of the stairs.

"What's wrong?"

"Hey, namesake," she said smiling.

Mamá took my schoolbag, dropped it by the stairs, and we went into the dining room.

"Did something happen?"

"No, nothing."

Lucila brought in my lunch and went back to the kitchen.

"How was your day today?"

"Fine," I said, waiting for her to give me the bad news any second. There'd been a nuclear bomb. Or worse. She'd announce she was leaving because papá was a monster, she had never wanted children, she was tired of her obligations, and Gonzalo was the one who made her happy.

"How would you like to spend your school holiday at a mountain house?"

"Is this what you were going to tell me?"

"Yes."

I exhaled.

"All three of us?"

"Of course."

"Does it have a pool?"

"It has a little waterfall, right on the terrace."

"Where is it?"

"Up in the mountains. Surrounded by cliffs like you wouldn't believe."

She said that while she'd been down in the shopping district paying some bills, she'd run into Mariú and Liliana, old classmates I'd never heard her talk about, and the two of them were going on vacation to Miami and renting out their second home.

"When we were girls, their mother disappeared there."

"What do you mean?"

"Poof, just vanished."

She was talking with the kind of excitement she'd been lacking for a long time, one that seemed particularly incongruous given what she was saying.

"I don't understand."

"It was a really misty night. She drove off in her car and never made it back, either to the mountain house or to her house in Cali. And no one ever saw her again."

I wanted to know exactly where she'd disappeared, when, how, why, and whether she was now in the Bermuda Triangle, but no matter what I asked, my mother said no more about it that day. She did, however, tell me that Mariú had two daughters and Liliana had one, that they were my age, and that I'd sleep in their room, which was full of toys. She also talked about the clothes we'd need. T-shirts for the daytime, since the sun was hot, sweaters for the night, when the fog came in, and rubber boots in case it rained.

"Help me convince your father tonight."

"You want us to go to *that* family's house?"

"Oh, Jorge, don't tell me you're going to make a stink over it."

"The lady who disappeared?" I asked.

They didn't even look at me, and she carried on recriminating.

"You'd say anything to stay home and not have to change a thing, wouldn't you?"

She began grasping at straws, saying that in Cali, with the guayacanes in full bloom, life was impossible for anyone with rhinitis. I turned to the balcony. The guayacanes were a wall of solid pink. It made no sense that she hadn't noticed them already. Now mamá was saying Mariú and Liliana had a relative that was a doctor, an allergist, and he'd recommended fresh mountain air.

"Which relative?" my father asked. "The uncle?"

"I don't know which relative, Jorge, they didn't say. But you know full well I've had no contact with anyone in that family for years."

Not understanding, I looked from one to the other. And then to Paulina, sitting in her place as though awaiting my explanation.

"You're truly going to refuse to let us go? You're going to condemn me to Cali? Don't you realize how sick I've been? I need a change, need to get out, do something, see some different scenery."

He stared at her and then finally conceded.

"The mountain air will do you good."

PART THREE

I SCRAPED BY in math, didn't have to take remedials, and passed the entire grade. At the end-of-year ceremony, I was congratulated. My mother and I packed our suitcases, and the following day we set out in the Renault 12, with papá at the wheel and the trunk packed full.

We drove down the avenue along the river and made a U-turn at the second bridge. After stopping at the gas station catty-corner from the supermarket to fill the tank, we got onto the coastal road. The higher we got, the more space there was between the houses, until there was more green than buildings, and Cali disappeared in the valley below.

I was kneeling and looking out the back window. Then I turned back around and sat next to Paulina. On a sharp curve, she fell over. I sat her back up. We passed cyclists, little houses, a church, more little houses and cyclists, and then, on the left-hand side, the mountain houses began. The scrubby vegetation was low and washed-out; the ground, orange. On the right, off in the distance, stood pointy mountains, and between us and them an abyss growing ever deeper.

"I feel queasy."

Mamá told me to open the window. The handle was hard to turn and I struggled with it, but in the end managed to get it down, and a sharp wind blew in.

"Do you need a bag?"

The road hugged the edge of the gorge. Only a few

spots, the most dangerous ones, had a guardrail, a tin barrier that might stop a bicycle at most.

"Claudia …"

"No."

"If you need to throw up, tell me."

I couldn't stop staring into the abyss.

"Claudia …"

"Okay."

The stairs in our apartment were a joke by comparison, the eighteen floors of Gloria Inés's house a trifle, and our car was kissing the precipice on every curve.

"What if we fall?"

"We're not going to fall."

In some places there were white crosses with bouquets of flowers, the names of the people who'd gone over and the dates of the accident.

"We'd die just like Princess Grace."

"We're not going to fall, child."

"Our car would be smashed up worse than hers."

"That's enough."

The houses, the bleached-out vegetation, the orange earth all stopped, and now on that side of the road was just a wall of creased, jagged gray rock. We came to Cerezo's Curve, the sharpest and longest of all, and papá had to drive very carefully, with both hands on the wheel. The dark precipice was the earth's open mouth. Paulina toppled over again, and when we came out of the curve I sat her up.

The incline softened, the vegetation turned to forest, and rather than cliffs now there were hills and plains, stands selling sheep's milk, roadside restaurants, mountain houses, and dirt-road turnoffs.

"How are you doing?" my mother asked.

"Okay."

"Not queasy anymore?"

"No."

Down in Cali it was a warm day, blue sky and tons of clouds. In the mountains it was cool, the sky was white, and though it was morning it looked almost like dusk. I wound the window up all the way. We passed the log-cabin restaurant where we'd stopped for arepas and aguapanela when we went to La Bocana with tía Amelia and Gonzalo.

My mother said it wasn't far to the turnoff, and that made it even longer. A couple of times my father asked if it was the next one. Mamá said no. At the highest point before the road began heading back down to the sea, she signaled.

"That way."

My father put on his blinker. We started down a narrow dirt road. Houses, restaurants, a forest of trees dripping with moss, like brontosauri chewing algae. All you could hear was the car's engine and the sound of pebbles as our tires kicked them aside. The forest opened onto a precipice even steeper than the one on the main road, darker and more terrifying. Then more forest on both sides, one final precipice, and then houses.

The country houses I'd been to were either old, colonial-style places with whitewashed walls and open breezeways, or flat, modest, mildew-smelling places.

This one looked like nothing special from the outside. A stone wall with a door in it. But we realized it was impressive the minute the caretaker opened the door. A rectangle wedged into the edge of the cliff, with humongous windows and views of the mountains and canyon.

Though it had been built years ago, the house was modern and had stylish floors and furniture, like the houses in Cali. At the same time, it was odd. The bedrooms were on the entry level, which was upstairs, on either side of a staircase with no banister that led down to the common areas, its steps jutting out of the stone wall like black piano keys.

My father and the caretaker went in first with the big suitcases. I carried Paulina in my arms and my backpack filled with other toys on my back. My mother, beside me, had her purse over one shoulder and a few shopping bags in her hands.

"This is the same style as our apartment, can you tell?"

"What do you mean?"

"The owner designed our building too. He's an architect."

"The disappeared lady's husband?"

Mamá's eyes lashed me like whips and then looked at the butler. His name was Porfirio, and he was young and light-skinned, with brown hair and small birdlike eyes set far apart. He wisely pretended not to have heard and carried the cases into the main room.

My father and Porfirio went to tour the property. My mother and I stayed in the main bedroom, her unpacking suitcases and me looking at everything.

The bed could fit four people, at least. The bathroom was like a whole other room, with three windows, two sinks, and a bathtub, and all of it white: the floor, the walls, the fixtures, the vases of flowers brought in from the garden. You could do a cartwheel in the closet and not bang into anything. The window in front of the bed was floor to ceiling and wall to wall.

I left Paulina on the bed, where my mother had placed the suitcases, and opened the gauze curtains and sliding doors. Suddenly the bedroom turned into a terrace. I went out and held on to the black steel banister, and a pin-like wind pricked my face.

The view was incredible. The canyon, wide and gaping, was blanketed in green forest, which grew darker the higher up the mountains it went. At the highest, most vertical drops, the forest disappeared and there was only bare rock, the shape and color of an old potato. And behind it, more and more blue mountain peaks in the distance, like a crested sea.

"I could have been Rebeca's sister-in-law," mamá said.

"Who?"

"The woman who disappeared."

I let go of the banister and turned around.

"What!"

"Your father hates the thought of me talking to you about it. He and your aunt say I give you too much information as it is."

"Please!" I begged.

She looked at me, trying to decide, and finally said, "I'm warning you, namesake: not a word to your father."

Rebeca, she told me, was the daughter of an Irish couple who'd emigrated to Cali after the First World War. The O'Briens. Their children were brought up like local Cali kids: they lived in San Fernando, supported Deportivo Cali, were members at the club. The four boys became swimmers. Rebeca, the only woman, was crowned queen of the club, and of the whole department.

"She was absolutely gorgeous. Tall and blonde, with blue eyes and a body to die for. A woman who stood out in Cali, where we're usually shorter and darker."

"Did you know her?"

"Of course I did. She was my friends' mother. Your grandmother, who went to school with her, said people used to stop what they were doing just to watch her go by. She was representing Cauca Valley in the National Beauty Contest but quit before she made it to Cartagena, to marry Fernando Ceballos, an architect from Bogotá who in Cali was making a name for himself; the runner-up ended up having to replace her."

Rebeca and Fernando, my mother continued, had two daughters, two cars, and two homes. They weren't good friends with my grandparents, but they'd see each other and say hello at the club and at parties. The Ceballos O'Briens lived in their Cali house, near the supermarket, during the week, a big house by the river. Weekends and holidays they spent at the mountain home.

It was a Saturday and they'd gone up early. They had lunch and spent the afternoon with the girls. That night they left them with the nanny and went to an anniversary party for some friends from the club. Their friends' house was in the village, below their house, less than ten minutes by car. Fernando's Land Rover was in the shop so they were in Rebeca's car, a dark-green Studebaker.

My grandparents were at that party and said that,

well into the night, after people had had a few drinks, my grandfather went out to smoke with some friends on the balcony.

Fernando and Rebeca were out there arguing. My grandfather and his friends saw her grab the keys from him and leave.

"Why were they fighting?"

"It seems he was a wild one."

"Wild how?"

Mamá put on a don't-be-naive-Claudia face and answered in a quiet voice, the voice she used for scandalous topics.

"He liked women."

"They were fighting because he was with someone else?"

"It wouldn't be surprising."

Solita de Vélez, my grandmother's friend, emerged from the bathroom just as Rebeca was walking out the door toward the parking lot.

"Where are you going?"

"Home."

"Are you alright?"

"Smashing."

Rebeca waved goodbye. She was in a white long-sleeved backless dress, her hair tied up with a ribbon. Outside the fog was so thick, Solita said, you could hardly see the fire from the torches.

"Drive carefully."

Rebeca kept walking toward the Studebaker and Solita stood watching until she got in, started the car, and the fog swallowed up first the car then the sound of the engine.

"Solita was the last person to see her."

"And that's where she disappeared?"

Mamá nodded.

"Fernando and her brothers searched the whole mountainside, with help from emergency workers, volunteers, and sniffer dogs. They never found signs of an accident."

"So it wasn't an accident."

"Fernando would get calls telling him they'd seen her at the airport, at a hotel, in some other city, another country ..."

"Calls from who?"

"Anonymous people. They'd say she was with a man."

"She ran off with someone else?"

"People talk a lot, Claudia. Maybe they just saw a blonde bombshell with blue eyes and thought it was her. Or they wanted the money. The family offered a reward for helping find her."

"And nobody did?"

"Nope. A psychic told Michael, the oldest brother, that Rebeca was alive but unable to return of her own free will, that she was in a faraway place, surrounded by water. Patrick, the youngest one, thought she'd gone to Ireland, the island their parents were from, so he set off to find her."

"But he didn't?"

"No."

My mother met Patrick far later, after he'd returned from Ireland and people in Cali no longer talked about Rebeca's disappearance or called Fernando Ceballos and gave him fake clues. They continued to talk about him, though, saying he was a lady's man, although no one ever met any official girlfriends nor did he ever remarry.

Patrick was thirty-four. He and his Irish wife separated, according to his nieces Mariú and Liliana, because she wanted to settle down and have children and all he wanted to do was go sailing. He had a yacht and had sailed all the way around Ireland. Now he was planning to sail the Caribbean, setting off from Cartagena, so in order to stay in shape he went swimming at the club.

This had been over the holidays. My mother was sixteen years old and spent all day sunbathing with Mariú and Liliana. Boys their age played tag, did cannonballs, and horsed around, while Patrick glided effortlessly through the water. When he finished, he'd swim to the edge of the pool, say hello, chat for a bit, make them laugh.

"He had copper-colored hair, a great tan, and blue eyes, like two gemstones in the desert. I thought he came over to talk to his nieces."

"But he didn't?"

"One day they weren't there and he came anyway: You can tell, can't you? he said. And I was like: Tell what? That it's for you. That what's because of me? Pretending I didn't get it, terrified it wasn't true."

From that day on they kept seeing each other out behind the club. I knew the place she meant. An unused clearing that had big trees, a place nobody ever went. Mariú and Liliana acted as accomplices, and sometimes Gloria Inés, who was already married and had just had her first child.

"You are one lucky duck, mija," she'd say to my mother as she burped or bottle-fed the baby.

Patrick regaled my mother with tales of his adventures at sea. The cold up north, real cold, not the slight chill they got in the Cali mountains. The storms. The raging seas. Days without enough food. The jobs he was forced to take at ports just to get by. He told her the good things too. The calm of the sea. That endless sea. The freedom.

She was dying for him to ask her to go with him, but he said he was sure a decent señorita like her was not cut out for that kind of life.

"It's clear you don't know me."

"Would you want to?" he asked in shock.

"Of course."

They started making plans to go off together. They'd sail the Caribbean, the Atlantic, the Mediterranean, all the seas. Visit the important ports as well as the ones no one in Cali had even heard of. Spend some time living in the fjords of Norway, in a fishing village on the Ivory Coast, on an island in the South Pacific ... One afternoon, very serious, he asked her if she wanted to have kids.

My mother stopped abruptly.

"And what did you say?" I asked.

She looked away, ashamed.

"I said no."

Now it was my turn to be the girl dripping water at the club, chest ripped open and her heart torn out.

"I was sixteen. I wasn't thinking about things like that. I was just a girl."

"Then what happened?"

Then Patrick went to speak to my grandfather and they locked themselves up in the study. My mother, all anxious, wanted to be in the living room so she could see their faces when they emerged. My grandmother told her that *that* wasn't the way a decent señorita comported herself, that she needed to show some dignity and self-respect, and my mother had to go to her room to wait. She waited and waited and, after an eternity, my grandmother came in.

"Claudia, I'm sorry."

Mamá thought she'd misheard, but my grandmother continued.

"Your father said no."

My mother remained silent. My grandmother sat down on the bed.

"What did you expect? The man is separated."

"I know, but ..."

"He was married by the Church. He can't divorce."

"We can still have a civil ceremony."

"How could you even think such a thing! Besides, he's not a professional, the man has no job, no money, no serious plans in life ..."

"He has a yacht, and we're going to sail the Caribbean."

My grandmother shook her head.

"And then around the world," she added.

"And what are you going to live off of? Tell me that."

"There're always jobs at ports."

My grandmother crossed her arms.

"Doing what?"

"In Ireland he worked cleaning ship engines."

"You want to marry a mechanic?"

"And there are taverns and inns."

"Oh, so a waiter."

"Patrick is an explorer."

"My God! What kind of life would he give you?"

"The kind I want."

"A life of struggle? Hunger? That's what you want?"

"No routine, no obligations, travel—that's what I want; freedom."

"Oh, child, you don't know what you're saying."

"I'm sixteen years old, I'm not a girl anymore."

"And he's thirty-four, far older than you."

"I like older men."

My grandmother stood. I pictured her, long and skinny, poised like a cobra.

"I know one day you'll see that he wasn't right for you," she said before walking out.

My mother stopped again.

"At that age," she explained, "you think you're grown up, but you're really not."

"Then what happened?"

The following day she met Patrick out behind the club and told him she was prepared to run off with him. He looked down.

"What's wrong?"

"Your father is right: this life is not for you."

He stroked her cheek and gave her a quick kiss. Then he turned and began walking away as she stood there, in a vacant lot surrounded by trees that kept it dark and shady so the grass wouldn't grow, watching him for the last time.

Gloria Inés, her baby over one shoulder, went to my mother. She put an arm around her and gave my mother her other shoulder to cry on.

Patrick went off to sail the Caribbean and my mother spent the rest of the year crying and furious with my grandparents, and then with Patrick for having obeyed them and not run off with her.

"I came down with a terrible case of rhinitis. I

couldn't sleep, couldn't eat, didn't go to school. I almost failed my next-to-last year of high school, and had to take remedial exams in three subjects."

The next year she found out Patrick had gotten married in Puerto Rico, to the daughter of an island woman and a gringo man, owners of a five-star beach hotel. She hated him. Hated his new wife. Hated people who found love and married, and decided to become a woman who didn't need anybody, a ruthless lawyer, but my grandfather refused to let her attend university.

Now I was the one stopping her.

"So when you said you wanted to go to university, you were mad."

"Furious."

My grandfather in his undershirt, big, hairy, and potbellied; and her defiant rather than meek: "I want to study at university."

My grandfather, shocked at the audacity.

"Law."

"University, law, my foot! What decent señoritas do is get married."

My mother not all little-girly but full of rancor, not shrinking but staring straight at him, hatred filling her lungs.

And then he died and left them bankrupt. My mother graduated from secondary school, had to move to a new neighborhood and upend her whole life, and never went back to the club or saw the Ceballos O'Brien sisters again. Gloria Inés, who did still go to the club, found out they were engaged to two brothers from Bogotá, architects like their father.

"They're getting married this year," she told my mother.

"I hope they don't invite me."

Gloria Inés, hands on her belly, expecting her second child, stared at her wide-eyed.

"Those girls are your school friends."

"*Were.* I never want to hear another word about them, about them or any other member of that family. Do you hear me?"

"And what did Gloria Inés say?"

"Nothing. She never mentioned them again, and they didn't invite me to their wedding."

"Do you think she told them not to?"

"Who knows."

"And you started volunteering at the hospital and met papá."

"Yep."

My mother grabbed a stack of clothes and put them in the closet. Paulina, sitting on the bed facing the window, seemed to be admiring the view. The pale sky and low clouds, lower than the mountains, moving so quickly it felt like it was the house that was moving instead. Mamá emerged from the closet.

"Was my grandmother right?"

"About what?"

"About you understanding one day that Patrick wasn't the one for you?"

She paused, confused. It was only a second, but felt as long as the years that had gone by since mamá got that lecture.

"Some things are best not to think about," she said.

She kept walking to the bed, pulled another stack of clothes out of the suitcases.

"And what do you think happened to Rebeca?"

"I think she wanted to disappear."

THE CLOUDS DISSOLVED from one minute to the next. The sun came out, the sky turned blue and everything came to life, like when someone takes an old black-and-white photo and turns it to color. The outline of mountains in the distance, the green of the forests, the flowers in the garden, the trees, and grass so perfect it looked plastic ...

Anita, the maid, served us lunch in the pergola. It was right next to the house and made of wrought iron. A big bougainvillea climbed one column, its trunk thick, heavy with purple blossoms, its branches extending over us like a roof. Lunch was beans and rice, fried pork belly, patacones, and avocado. Anita was white, like her husband, and had curly black hair and a shy smile for everything.

"Thank you, Anita."

Shy smile.

"Delicious beans."

Shy smile.

Anita left us, and my father put his hand on top of mother's.

"Are you happy?"

The sun filtered through the bougainvillea branches. Two red butterflies and a tiny hummingbird flitted around the flowers. The stream that ran through the property, its water trickling down through the rocks, tinkled like little bells.

"Very," she said, with a look that took in the

nature as well as the buildings. "Isn't this place amazing?"

"Yes," I said.

Paulina, sitting there with us at the table, her back to the precipice, with her placid little face and curly eyelashes, looked as pleased as I was.

That afternoon, Porfirio came down to the house to close the giant windows.

"Keep the cold from getting in."

No sooner had he said it than it got in. A damp kind of cold that made our clothes and everything else, even the air we breathed, feel heavy. We were in the living room. My father was reading the paper. My mother, a magazine. I was on the floor at the center table, on a cushiony long-haired rug, working on a two-thousand-piece jigsaw puzzle I'd found in the study: a European landscape with a pond, a windmill, and horses.

"Would you like me to light a fire?" Porfirio asked.

"Please," said mamá.

My father went into the back room with Porfirio and the two of them set to work. My mother said it was time for us to put on our sweaters. She set down her magazine and went upstairs. I was planning to follow, but as soon as I stood and looked up, I became hypnotized. Now it really was almost dusk.

The sky had clouded over, and dense fog hung, floating at the tops of the mountains. A white amoeba-shaped blob. I watched it expand, advance, approach the house and then envelop it, as though refusing to stay outside, searching for gaps in the doors or other holes it could slip through.

Outside everything was white, while inside it turned to darkness.

"Didn't you go get your sweater?" asked mamá, coming back with hers on.

The house, encased in fog, was transformed. Narrow and flat, like a fake house on TV.

"Get going," she insisted.

I went upstairs and put on my sweater. The girls' room was big. It had three beds, each up against a different wall, in U-formation. Two trunks, between the beds, served as nightstands. There were shelves full of dolls, toys, and *Children's World* encyclopedias. I grabbed the *Amazing Places* volume and sat down on the bed.

In it I saw a statue larger than any building of a naked man with his ding-dong out. I saw pyramids, hanging gardens, a hut floating on a river, waterfalls, geysers, volcanos, snowy peaks, skyscrapers, palaces, and temples. My mother called me to the table and I went downstairs with Paulina.

It was dark out.

All the lights in the house were on. Porfirio had left and the chimney was blazing in the back room. The fire and lights were reflected in the windows. Everything else was black, and it was as if the only thing in the whole world was that house, a solitary planet out in space.

My father was in the dining room, his back to the tallest window. I put Paulina at the head of the table and sat down beside her. Mamá was making dinner in the open kitchen. Her hair reached halfway down her back. It was straight and shiny; she must have brushed it when she went up for her sweater, and it made me want to stroke it. She raised the top of the waffle iron, pulled out a couple of steaming sandwiches, brought them to the table, and sat down across from my father. He poured the orange juice.

"How old were Mariú and Liliana when their mother disappeared?"

My parents exchanged a look.

"You've been talking about that?"

"Put down the juice, Claudia," mamá said. "Eat your sandwich first."

"It's not an appropriate topic for her."

"What do you want me to do? Hide it from her? Lie?"

"How old were they?" I insisted.

He shook his head. She tried to remember.

"I think Mariú and I were in third grade. Liliana was a year younger."

"So, eight?"

"About that," she confirmed. "We were the same age as you, and Rebeca the same age as me."

"Then Paulina was right: she didn't want to disappear."

"Paulina told you that?"

Chewing, I said yes.

"She talks now?"

"Yes, and she said that a mother would never abandon her daughters, especially if they were little."

My parents glanced at one another. Then at Paulina, at the head of the table, perfect in her green dress and with hair like mamá's.

"Since when does she talk?"

"Since we got here."

The following morning, my father had already left for the supermarket when I woke up. Since he had to take the mountain road, he left earlier than he did in Cali, and since I was on vacation, I slept later. I ate breakfast with mamá and then we opened the giant windows. The sky was clean and clear, as if somebody had shined it. Soon the sun came up over the mountaintops and the cold broke. We put on our bathing suits and went out to our private waterfall, on the terrace on one side of the house.

The terrace was enormous, with a stone floor and a black steel railing at the precipice. It had the same view as the main bedroom. Sky, canyon, forest, mountains. But this was wide open, no walls or roof, which made it more imposing. People—us—in that landscape, were like nothing, little cardboard figures, tiny dots in the immensity of it all.

Our waterfall was made of stone. Porfirio opened the sluice that let in water from the stream, and it came gushing forcefully out. He left, and mamá and I lay out on chaises, her with an issue of *¡Hola!* and an iraca palm frond to protect her from the sun's rays.

We stayed silent for a while, just toasting in the sun. Then she said something I couldn't hear with all the noise from the waterfall.

"What?"

"I said, she liked to drink."

On the cover of the magazine, a bride and groom, Paquirri and Isabel Pantoja. Him with dimples, green eyes, and a bullfighter's suit; her with jet-black hair, a layered white veil, and a diamantine tiara.

"Who did?"

"Rebeca. At the club, you'd always see her with a drink. The girls would be in the pool, and her with a glass of white wine."

"Was she drinking that night?"

"The night she disappeared? Of course she was, Claudia, don't be so naive. Probably something strong too. At night, she drank whisky, according to the lulo-club ladies."

I felt like I was on fire. The heat in the mountains was nothing like the heat in Cali, in the lowlands. Here it stung like hot pepper. I got up and, without thinking or even feeling it first, stepped into the waterfall. It felt like my head was going to explode, my bones were turning to jelly. Standing under the waterfall was like shouting into a forsaken land, a cold desert, a barren plain.

My father didn't come back for lunch. It was too hard to drive down and back two times in one day, so on weekdays and Saturdays, while we were at the mountain house, he had lunch at tía Amelia's.

Anita served mamá and me in the dining room. Shy smile. When we were finished, we tried to clear our plates and take them to the kitchen, but she wouldn't let us.

My mother suggested we go for a walk. In Cali she never came with my father and me, so I looked at her in shock.

"What's so odd about that?" she said.

We put on blue jeans, T-shirts, and rubber boots and tied sweaters around our waists in case it clouded over. We climbed up the driveway, opened the black steel gate, and set out on the unpaved road.

We walked slowly, looking at the houses. There were all kinds, old and new, brick and wood, with big windows and small ones, peaked roofs and flat. And they had gardens full of flowers and fruit trees, pinewood fences, and dogs that barked or wagged their tails at us from within.

We came across another couple, a group of old men in hats with canes, a peasant carrying a heavy load on his shoulders, and a bunch of kids out partying, with a giant boom box blaring music in English, passing around a bottle of aguardiente.

We saw a flock of green parakeets with blue marks around their eyes, a lone cow grazing in a treeless plot, and two gorges with giant rocks and water loud as an angry mob.

We came to a swathe of forest where the world went dark. It had trees laden with moss, plants with giant leaves, fallen tree trunks rotting on the ground, and a lamppost covered in rust-orange fuzz. Then came a curve, and at the end of the curve, a precipice. We approached. Slowly. Unsure of ourselves. A few scraggy trees clung to the rock face and then immediately the ground fell away, as though it had been hacked off with a machete.

I felt tiny: the baby staring down our apartment stairs from the security gate, but now without the guardrail. Just me, with nothing but my body, at the face of an actual cliff. The canyon was narrow there, and down below, where the streams and gullies all met, the river was covered in vegetation: an untamed jungle.

I thought about all the dead women. Staring out over the precipice was looking into their eyes. Into the eyes of Gloria Inés, haughty as a horse and then splattered on the sidewalk. I looked at my mother, leaning over the abyss like me.

"We better go back."

On the property, the house and terrace—the giant windows and railings—acted as protection. There was only one place outside that directly overlooked the abyss, with nothing but a wood fence for protection. It was over by the eucalyptus trees that bordered the neighbors' property, close to their stables. When we got back, mamá went straight into the house. I stayed out, staring at the unprotected area.

The fence was low, barely even up to my chest, and didn't look very strong. Just a few wood planks. The void, two steps away, had no trees blocking it. I walked over, feeling reserved at first, and then determined. I wanted to face the abyss again, to feel the luscious feeling in my belly, and the fear, the desire both to jump and to run away. Porfirio, who was raking fallen leaves, dropped his rake and ran to me.

"It's best if you don't go over there," he said, panting. "That fence isn't safe. The wood rots and we keep having to replace it."

I stopped. Looked at him.

"We don't want you falling over the cliff, do we?"

I saw my body plunging into the green nothingness below.

"No."

"If you want to go to the stables I can take you."

He must have thought I wanted to see the horses, that that was what had attracted me.

"You just let me know and we can go take the out-side route, along the road, not through."

I nodded, still consumed by the vision of my fall.

Late that afternoon Porfirio came down to close the giant windows and light a fire. Just like the day before, fog engulfed the house from outside, but this time instead of dense it was wispy, like a veil.

The house was silent. It was like being in a fish-bowl. It wouldn't have surprised me if a huge eye-ball peered in to look at us.

Porfirio left, my mother and I put on our sweaters, and she lay on the sofa reading the same copy of *¡Hola!* with Paquirri and Isabel Pantoja. I started back on the jigsaw, and when I looked up it was night.

"What time will papá get back?"

My mother looked at her watch.

"We're forty minutes from Cali, but at this time of day and with that fog ..."

The fire and lights from the house were reflected in the window. Everything else was darkness. My father was out there, in the black of that world, driv-ing in the fog on a narrow road full of dangerous curves.

"What if he has an accident?"

"He's not going to have an accident."

"What if he disappears like Rebeca?"

"He's not going to disappear, child."

She got up to make dinner. I stood too, and sat Paulina at the table.

"Next week there's a training course and he'll be leaving even later. You have to calm down."

We had pita-bread pizzas and went into the room with the fireplace. My mother took a bottle of whisky from the bar and poured herself a drink. She was not one to drink anything alone, much less whisky.

"What are you looking at?" she asked, taking a sip.

My father got home when I was going to bed. He came into my room and told me tía Amelia had sent me a kiss, and gave me two.

"Was there fog on the road?"

"Lots."

"Did you drink wine with tía Amelia?"

"No."

"You have to drive carefully."

"I know."

The following morning I didn't see him at all. It was a cold, melancholy day. Everything covered in clouds. The sky, the canyon, the mountainside. The peaks looked like islands in a white lagoon.

My mother and I couldn't take off our sweaters or go in the waterfall. We were bored all morning, ate lunch, and were still bored in the afternoon, until Porfirio asked if we wanted to go see the neighbors' horses. I looked at mamá, excited.

"Alright," she said.

The owners weren't there. The caretaker was a friend of Porfirio's. A skinny guy, with a soggy cigarette in his mouth and an Adam's apple big as a second nose.

"Are you going to ride?" he asked.

I said yes and my mother said no.

"Pretty please."

"It's no trouble?" she asked the caretaker.

"No, señora."

He saddled up three horses. Brown ones for them and a palomino mare for me. We rode along the unpaved road, looking down on the world from up high, and I felt powerful, like the princess of an ancient kingdom. We got back to the house all muddy and smelling like horse: straight to the shower. Then I changed right into my pajamas and went downstairs with Paulina.

Porfirio was working on the fireplace. I told him about my ride. That my horse had a long mane and eyelashes, that she sneezed and got disgusting green snot on my pants, that at a house with a blue roof some Doberman Pinschers ran at us, barking and furious, like on *Magnum PI*.

"Good thing the horses didn't spook, or kick them."

"Oh, they're nice and tame," he said. "Only thing they're afraid of is Old Viruñas."

"Who's that?"

Old Viruñas, he told me, was a devil who lived on people's property, inside their houses, but not this side, behind the walls. He slept by day and woke at night. The strange noises, the ones you didn't know where they were coming from—stuff that sounded like birds on the roof, or the wood creaking, or air in the pipes—he made by scratching the guts of the house.

"Why does he scratch the guts?"

"To get out."

"And does he?"

"Oh, he does," Porfirio assured me. "He eats fog to stay alive."

I pictured him all slippery and bald. A demon with poppy-out eyes and gnarled fingernails who made himself flat to fit through the cracks and snatched clumps of fog and stuffed them into his mouth like cotton candy.

"He's the one who braids horses' tails and scratches people while they sleep. Haven't you ever woken up with scratch marks you didn't have when you went to bed?"

I didn't know what to say.

"That's why I sleep with one eye open," he said.

"Porfirio, don't go scaring the girl with those old stories!" mamá chided, walking down the stairs.

"Sorry, señora."

But it was too late. Porfirio said goodbye and I sat down in front of the jigsaw puzzle. I had organized the pieces by color and put together a few sections of the sky and pond. Nothing of the windmill. I still thought there might be an Old Viruñas living in there, scratching the wood and making the horses whinny, so it seemed best to go to the kitchen.

"Mamá, does Old Viruñas really exist?"

"Of course not."

"What time is papá coming home?"

"Not for a while."

One morning, I didn't find my mother downstairs in the kitchen having coffee, as had become the custom. I went upstairs. She had the curtains open, the room was bright, and she was lying face-up in bed, motionless, as if floating on water.

"You're awake," she said.

She got up. Put on her white bathrobe. Went

downstairs and made me breakfast. After waiting for me to finish eating, she took the plate to the kitchen and headed for the stairs.

"Don't you want to go to the waterfall?"

We went whenever weather permitted and were both now darker than Sophia Loren.

"No."

"But look at the sun."

It was high in the sky, pouring down over the mountains like lava.

"I don't feel like it today."

Mamá went back to how she was in Cali. Spending all day in bed, with or without a magazine, staring at the ceiling or walls.

At night she'd make me dinner and pour herself a whisky. I tried to wait up for my father, since I couldn't relax until I heard his car coming down the driveway, but she was strict: at eight o'clock on the dot she sent me to bed, and sleep almost always overtook me before he got home.

The days became long, and I spent them wandering the property.

I'd roam the grounds, which were always perfect. The short-cut grass, the pine-log fence, the plants in bloom, the piles of leaves Porfirio assembled with his rake.

I'd climb up the driveway, popping the seed pods from the impatiens planted on either side between my fingers as I went. Poking the touch-me-nots so they'd close up. Gathering petals, leaves, sticks, and rocks and making compositions in the grass.

Climbing the prettiest tree, a carbonero pittieri with long white wisps, low branches, and rough bark that was easy to peel.

I watched the ants climbing up its trunk and the birds perched on its branches. Looked for nests. Chased grasshoppers and butterflies. Caught the frogs living in the plants, under their leaves, and held them for a while before setting them free.

I tromped through the brook in my rubber boots, upstream and downstream, trying in vain to keep my boots from filling with water. I didn't want to have to put on my suede yellow-striped Adidas since I hated getting them dirty. I peeled white lichens off the rocks to see the tiny creatures living underneath. Wet my hair and face and cupped my hands to drink from them.

I took orange dirt from the borders. Made cakes and decorated them with sticks, rocks, and leaves. Took black dirt from the garden and frosted the cakes with it, like chocolate. Served them to Paulina, and we pretended they were delicious and we were gobbling them up.

I slid down hills on a piece of cardboard, careful not to get close to the unprotected area with the flimsy fence that Porfirio had warned me about. I just looked at it from afar.

In one of the trunks in the girls' room, along with tons of other stuff, I found a set of pewter dishes, like real ones but doll-sized. I stuck them in my backpack, grabbed Paulina, and set off on an excursion.

We got to the pinewood fence up by the road, at the upper edge of the property. A few days earlier

I'd discovered a natural arch there that looked like a gnomes' house. It had a dirt floor, and a back wall formed by the pine tree's trunk and branches. The side walls and ceiling were dense, green, and rough.

Ducking to enter, I sat down and inhaled so the smell would fill my lungs. It smelled fresh, like an icy cocktail of mint and lemon. After setting Paulina down, I took off my backpack, pulled out the dishes, and organized them.

Right when I began pouring invisible tea I felt something on me. A long strip I thought was an overgrown branch. I went to pull it aside, but looking up I saw that it was in front of me and realized it was a snake. Its body was inside the weave of the tree, its head hanging down. With its V-shape tongue, the snake was flicking the air, no doubt detecting my presence.

I ran to the caretakers' cabin, which, like the big house, was a stone rectangle with a door in it, but in miniature. The door was open.

"There's a snake!"

Everything—the kitchen, the double bed, the dining-room table—was crammed into the same space. A room with no partitions, no windows, no view, the size of the main bedroom's closet in the big house. There were no decorations, no paintings. Just stone walls, a door that must have been to a bathroom, and a few shiny pots and pans hanging by the stove. Anita was sweeping, Porfirio, eating soup.

"Where?" he asked, dropping his spoon.

"In the arch," I pointed. "It was on top of me!"

Porfirio stood, put on his rubber boots, and grabbed his machete. Anita dropped her broom and came out with us.

The snake was still where I left it. Porfirio reached the machete in. Calmly, he coaxed it onto the blade, as far from his hand as possible, then drew the machete out. Anita and I looked on from a distance. On the machete blade, it looked like rubber, a prank snake.

I don't know why I thought Porfirio was going to hurl it off the property, over the fence. Instead, he put it on the ground and, before it could get away, in one quick, innocent little move, chopped off its head. The machete sank into the earth and the headless body squirmed.

"It didn't die."

"Oh, it's dead," Porfirio said.

"But it's moving."

The head was off to one side, the body still coiling around.

"Wait and see."

I looked at Anita, for once not wearing her shy smile. She nodded.

Finally the snake grew still. Behind it, in the arch, were the cups and plates, the overturned teapot, and Paulina, fallen on her side, eyes wide open as though staring at the snake. It was skinny, barely longer than my arm, and had bright bands of black, orange, and white, a thing of beauty with an amputated head.

"Coral snake. A redtail, very poisonous," Porfirio said. "You saved yourself from a bite."

Porfirio disposed of the body, hurling it over the cliff. Anita and I watched it twist in the air and then disappear into the abyss. He stood at the edge of the fence; the two of us farther back, with Anita protecting me. This was the closest I'd been to that place and, pressing Paulina to my body, I felt woozy but also got the luscious feeling in my belly.

Overexcited, I ran into the big bedroom.

"A redtail almost bit me."

Mamá was in bed with a magazine.

"What's that?"

"A really poisonous snake."

My chest was heaving.

"Oh," she said, turning back to her magazine.

"Porfirio chopped its head off with a machete."

I was standing by her bed, waiting for her to ask how I'd escaped, whether I was sure I was okay, waiting for her to show some alarm, examine me. Both of us were peeling and our arms and faces had lighter patches of skin with the edges curled up.

Nothing. She kept reading.

In the study, which was on the first floor between the living room and the fireplace room, there was a wall-to-wall bookcase filled with novels, encyclopedias, and books on art, design, and architecture.

One afternoon when it was raining drops fat as stones, I spent the day looking at the books of photos and illustrations. I saw country houses, beach houses, city houses, brightly colored plastic furniture, building blueprints, aerial photos, paintings, drawings, nudes. The rain—with no wind or lightning—sounded smooth, and the giant window misted up. I got cold and went for a sweater.

My mother, curled up in bed, was sleeping.

I went back to the study. Climbed the bookcase to get a red book down from the top shelf. When I tugged on it, an envelope full of photos fell, spilling out onto the floor. I forgot about the book and sat down to look at them. They were color, recent, Semana Santa was my guess, when me and my parents were home bored in our apartment.

The whole family was in them. A man with white hair who must have been Fernando Ceballos, his daughters Mariú and Liliana, their husbands, the girls. Most of them were of the girls. Under the waterfall, on the chaises in the sun, at a picnic with mud pies, climbing the wispy carbonero tree, on the neighbors' horses, with their dolls and the pewter dish set—just like me, basically.

There was one of them in the countryside, standing in front of a rustic shop with log walls and soft-drink posters. The three of them in bootcut jeans, their hair in two pigtails, so blonde it was almost white, holding purple Sandy sundaes. Another photo, closer up, showed their light eyes and lips all red, no doubt from the Sandys, which were icy.

They were so pretty.

My mother could have been their tía. An adventurous aunt, childless and in love with her husband and satisfied with her life, an aunt who adored her nieces and brought back presents for them from her trips to places all over the world. The kind of woman those girls—all girls—wanted to be when they grew up. All you'd have to do was tell them tía Claudia was coming to visit and they'd be unable to sleep till she got there.

"Tíatíatíatíatía."

Excited not for the presents but because they loved her more than Uncle Patrick, even if he was their blood relative and she was the in-law. Tía Claudia, with dark hair and dark eyes, so different from them but so beautiful in her own way.

"My girls."

She'd bend down to embrace them.

I didn't know when it stopped raining, because the giant window was still all misty. I got up, went over, and wiped a finger across the glass, leaving a fat stripe. Then I used my whole hand and rubbed hard, side to side, from the floor to as high as I could, on tiptoes and stretching up my arm, until the whole thing, except the highest part that was out of reach, was clear.

Outside, the glass was covered in tiny droplets that made the world look distorted, like when I put on my father's glasses. A mishmash of shapeless colors and, in the distance, brightness: the sun, making a breakthrough.

I had to go to the log-cabin store with soft-drink posters in my bootcut jeans and my hair in two pigtails, even if they weren't blonde and I didn't have light eyes, to buy a purple Sandy sundae and suck it till my lips froze.

"Porfirio, do you know of a shop that sells Sandys?"

The sun was shining like it hadn't even rained. Thick steam rose off the still-wet grass.

"Almost every shop in town."

He was crouched down, planting daisies around a tree.

"I don't feel like going into town. Isn't there one out here?"

"Far as I know, the school shop has them."

The school shop, which I'd seen from horseback, was a metal hut.

"That's it?"

He thought a minute.

"I think there's one higher up, too, past the turnoff to town."

"Is it metal like the school shop?"

"It's a big place, made of logs."

"Can you take me there?"

"If your mother has no problem with it ..."

Porfirio kept planting daisies and after a minute looked at me with an odd expression.

"The other day the guerrillas were there."

"Guerillas?"

"Young kids. They robbed a milk truck on the main road and gave all the milk to the people in the village."

"Really?"

"Didn't charge a single peso."

It was clear I didn't believe him.

"Honest," he said. "Don't you know they take from the rich to give to the poor?"

"Like Robin Hood?"

Mamá was reading *Cosmopolitan*, lying on the sofa in the fireplace room, her hair cascading down like a waterfall.

"Porfirio's going to take me to a shop that sells Sandys."

No reaction.

"I'm going to get a purple one."

She grunted in a way that could have meant anything.

"So I can go?"

Nothing.

"Mamá?"

Nothing.

"Mamá!"

"What?"

"I said, can I go?"

She set her magazine down and looked at me.

"Go where?"

"I just said, to a store that sells Sandys."

"It's too late for that now, Claudia."

She sat up and grabbed a glass from the floor. It was whisky, at that hour, the middle of the day; before my afternoon snack, even.

"I said tomorrow, me and Porfirio."

"Fine."

She drank.

"You're drinking, now?"

"Have you got a problem with it?"

I chose not to reply.

"It's a log-cabin shop."

She set the glass down and lay down with her magazine.

"Great."

"Porfirio said the guerillas were there the other day."

"Imagine."

"Young boys."

"Mmm."

"They robbed a milk truck and gave it all to the poor."

She dropped the magazine onto her chest.

"He said what?"

"The guerrillas are like Robin Hood."

"The guerrillas are bad."

She flipped the magazine shut and sat up.

"Porfirio told me that ..."

"Porfirio thinks Old Vicuñas exists. Porfirio is an ignoramus and you can't believe a word he says, Claudia. The guerrillas want to make us like Cuba."

"What's wrong with Cuba?"

"In Cuba they tell children to ask God for ice cream, and since God doesn't bring it to them, they tell them to ask Fidel."

My mother picked up her whisky and downed it.

"And Fidel brings it?"

She wiped her mouth.

"They take everything away from people. Their homes, their land, their businesses. They'd take this house away from Mariú and Liliana, take the supermarket away from us."

"Because they want to share everything with the poor?"

"Because they want to make everyone poor."

She stood, went to the bar, and poured herself another whisky.

"I don't want you speaking to Porfirio anymore."

I saw that her nose was red.

"Why?"

"How many times do I have to tell you, Claudia?"

And her voice stuffed up. "You shouldn't befriend the help."

"Because they leave?"

"And because they say idiotic things."

"Is your rhinitis back?"

"No."

"Were you crying?"

She shrugged.

That night I promised myself I'd wait up for my father.

It got late, and I started to feel like an orphan. If he'd gone over the cliff, I would actually be one, like him. Then I heard the sound of a car engine coming down the driveway. It was him. I turned on the light and, when he came into my room, hugged him.

"I want a new mother."

"What's wrong with yours?"

"Everything."

"Did you have a fight?"

"She won't let me go with Porfirio to buy Sandys."

"She must have her reasons, Claudia."

Furious with him too now, I turned my back and went to bed.

WHEN SHE WAS in bed or lying on the sofa, mamá was annoyed by everything. Like me talking.

"You simply cannot keep your mouth shut, can you?"

Or if I kept my mouth shut, by me moving or walking around.

"Would you sit still, child?"

Or if my mouth was shut and I sat still, making every effort to go unnoticed, my very presence annoyed her.

"Why don't you go outside, or to your room?"

At lunchtime Anita bustled around in the kitchen. In the afternoon, Porfirio closed the big windows and lit a fire. When he left, mamá would get up to make a snack. This was the one time you could talk to her.

"Do you remember the day Rebeca disappeared?"

And that was the one topic that hooked her in.

"Not the exact day, no."

Sometimes she'd tell me things.

"I remember Mariú and Liliana stopped going to school for a while."

"How long?"

Sometimes she lost patience quickly.

"I don't know, Claudia. A week, a month, a while."

And I'd drop it.

One night I got her to tell me that, after a while, the Head of Discipline, a round old nun, came into their classroom to tell them that Mariú and Liliana would be returning the following day and they were not to ask any inappropriate questions, which meant any questions about their mother's disappearance.

"And they came back?"

"Same as ever. Their hair in two braids, no sign they'd been crying, no bags under their eyes, nothing."

"Did you say anything to them?"

"I didn't, but one of my friends put a hand on Mariú's shoulder and said she was sorry."

"And what did she do?"

"Nothing."

"She didn't cry?"

"No, and at recess she told me she knew her mother was still alive."

I opened my eyes wide.

"She told you that?"

"Yep."

"What did you say?"

Mamá made a sweeping gesture with her hand that could have meant anything, that she didn't remember or didn't want to talk about it anymore, and I left it there.

While we were eating, she went back to the topic, without my asking. The reason she didn't talk to Mariú, she said, was because the sisters were so close, and you couldn't talk to Mariú without Liliana—who was reserved and evasive—being there too. Then she chewed in silence for a while. Finally she added that the only reason she'd heard the rumors was because the card-club ladies talked of nothing else.

"What did they say?"

"What didn't they say, child."

And that was it.

She started on the whisky early the next afternoon. On her second one, she got chatty while buttering rolls and told me what the card-club ladies said.

That the man Rebeca ran off with must have been important, a millionaire, powerful, a TV star. That she could never handle her drink. That her husband couldn't stand her. That she hadn't disappeared, she'd been locked up. That she was the one who couldn't stand her husband. That she'd jumped off the cliff, shattered by all his infidelities. That she hadn't taken her children into consideration. That her body was rotting in some forest so dense you couldn't see the car, which was the same green as the vegetation. That the campesinos had begun seeing a woman in white with blonde hair and light eyes. Rebeca O'Brien, a ghost in the mist. That she'd always been a modern woman, wore low-cut dresses and didn't take her husband's name, so unlike her parents, born-and-bred Irish, observant Catholics. That a bunch of liberals she met on those walks she took in the mountains had finally brainwashed her and she was off in the jungle, a pants-wearing outlaw, rifle across her chest. That she'd been kidnapped. That the Monster of the Magones—a Cali serial killer back then—had gotten her. That there'd been sightings, that she was abducted. That there had been cases of people lost in the fog who later turned up on different continents. That she had amnesia and didn't remember a thing, not where she was from, who she was, or that she had two little girls.

I hadn't told my mother or anyone else about the photos. I suppose I didn't want them to be taken away. I left the envelope where I'd found it, up on the top shelf, on the red book.

Then I thought someone might find it. Anita, maybe, when she was cleaning. So to keep it from being seen, I slipped it inside the book. When nobody was around, I'd take it down and gaze at the photos.

There was one of Mariú and Liliana standing outside the house, before the stone facade, with the girls in front of them. Five tall, healthy-looking, light-eyed blondes. The girls had two braids each, like their mothers must have worn when they were little. The mothers wore their hair down, one straight with bangs like Bo Derek, the other with feathered layers like Farrah Fawcett. Smiling into the camera as if they'd suffered no misfortune at all.

Mamá and I had finished peeling and returned to our original color when she said, "Remember that time we bumped into Mariú and Liliana at the shopping center?"

"Nooooo! I know them?"

"You must have been three or four, we only saw them briefly. You were a mess, since you could never sit still for a second. Covered in dirt, or chocolate or something, with your short, urchin hair that refused to grow. While they, of course, looked just divine. Beautiful dresses, long hair, like they were off to a party. The girls and their mothers both. They were something, those women," she sighed, "like two dolls. Maríu said you were pretty, she's always been so generous."

My mother got up, took the dishes to the sink and went into the fireplace room. I stayed in the dining room with Paulina, picked her up and examined her carefully. Chocolate-brown hair, blue eyes, thick lashes, a pointy nose, and full lips. The prettiest doll ever. It wasn't just me who thought so. Tía Amelia and mamá did too. Gloria Inés said so when she saw her. My school friends say so, and Doña Imelda, and my art teacher. Even Lucila and papá, who barely even spoke.

I went into the fireplace room to see what my mother was up to. She was sitting on the sofa, staring at the fire, a whisky in her hands.

I went into the study. Taking out the photos, I started examining the Ceballos O'Brien's the same way I had Paulina. I wanted to understand what my mother meant, the quality of their beauty, if they really were dolls. Like Paulina, they had light eyes, pointy noses, and full lips. You couldn't see their eyelashes or the exact color of their eyes, and maybe their hair wasn't as full or as long, but they were tall, blonde, and curvy, and now I had no doubt. They were prettier, far prettier, than the prettiest doll ever.

I couldn't stop staring at those photos. Every day. It was like I wanted to scratch the surface, their beauty, and see what was underneath, the pain and orphanhood.

Of the five, the one with Bo Derek hair was the most beautiful. And the tallest. A stylized woman, with the perfect features of a sculpture.

"Who's prettier, Mariú or Liliana?"

It was a cold Sunday afternoon and the three of us were in the living room, windows closed, sweaters on. My father was reading the paper and my mother, a whisky in hand, was staring out the window.

"Some people say Liliana, but to me it's Mariú."

I was sitting on the floor, working on the jigsaw. The horses were complete. And I'd done large parts of the meadow, the pond, and the sky. The windmill, where the landscape was darker, was the only part with holes in it.

"What does Mariú look like?"

My mother didn't reply.

"Mamá ..."

"Tall, good cheekbones, gray eyes. I remember they used to change color, get darker and lighter, depending on the weather, her clothes, her mood."

"Taller than Liliana?"

"Yes."

"I think I'd think she was prettier too."

And a good mother, though I didn't say that part out loud. A mother who let her daughters go get Sandys and thought I was pretty.

"Look at that storm," mamá said.

"What storm?" papá replied, glancing up.

She pointed to the farthest mountains and then I saw it in the distance: a black stain pouring down on the earth, and sudden yellow flashes.

One of the photos was of Mariú and a man with dark, messy hair. Her husband, I assumed. He was gazing at her as if she was the most important thing in the whole universe. Mariú, shy, eyes lowered, was smiling.

In another, which must have been taken right after, her face filled the frame. She stared right into the camera, so it was as if she was looking at me. Her eyes were amazing. Light, and maybe sad. Was the sadness for her disappeared mother? Did she still feel the sorrow of her absence? Did it still hurt? Had that grief trailed behind her like a comet's tail since she was eight?

Nowhere in the house were there photos or portraits of Rebeca. I searched the bedrooms, the closets, the drawers, and the books in the library, one by one, in case a photo had been forgotten. I found none.

The wall across from the desk had a series of pictures. Illustrations, scenes of everyday life. A movie theater, a dance, a bridge, a woman standing at an open door, facing away from the camera. She wore a long low-backed dress, had blonde shoulder-length hair, and held a glass of something yellow.

I went in to tell my mother I'd found a picture of Rebeca. She looked at me, trying to ascertain whether it was true. When I continued giving her a serious look, she put down her magazine and got up.

"Pff, that's obviously not her."

"But she's wearing white, holding a drink, leaving the party."

"It's just a drawing, Claudia."

"Of the night she disappeared."

"How on earth could you think they would put a picture of the night she disappeared up on the wall?" she said, her voice making clear that she'd had enough of my stupidity.

On another night, I discovered—using a magnifying glass I'd found in the desk—that in the photo of Mariú looking at the camera, you could see the photographer reflected in her eyes.

Given the shape—svelte, big hair—I was convinced it was Liliana. Beside this reflection was a lighter spot, or maybe something shining, that could have been anything—the floor lamp in the study, the coatrack at the front door, a person, a curtain. But I had a feeling it was Rebeca, floating there in her white dress.

That was when my fear truly took hold.

I put the photo back and, on my way to the door, avoided looking at the picture of the woman's back, afraid she might turn around and I'd see that she had no face: just a skull with empty eye sockets.

I saw my reflection in the horizontal mirror in the hall on my way past, and it was as if it wasn't me. As if it was some independent *thing*. Hunched, slippery, emaciated, Old Viruñas who lived in the walls and had now come out.

Logs were burning in the fireplace. Mamá, her face bathed in the orange glow of the fire, was pouring herself another whisky. Seeing me, she looked at her watch.

"It's time for bed."

"When papá gets back."

"Not this again."

"Please, mamá."

She said no, but whisky softened her up and I convinced her to come up to my room. She stayed with me while I changed into my pajamas, positioned Paulina in the bed on the opposite wall, and got into my own, against the wall with the door.

"Will you tell me a story?"

"What are you, three?"

"Just stay till my bed warms up."

The sheets were cold as a lizard's belly.

"Goodnight, Claudia."

She turned out the light. The room wasn't entirely dark because I left the curtain open so the light from the lamppost by the fence, at the cliff, would come in.

"Paulina wanted me to ask you to sleep in here with us."

"You don't say."

"You could sleep in that bed."

I pointed to the empty one on the back wall.

"Tell her thank you very much, but I can't leave the fire unattended."

"She can hear you, mamá."

"Well, then she knows."

She closed the door from the outside and went downstairs. The sound of footsteps, muffled by wool socks. The silence growing deeper and deeper, as if the house were sinking with every step she descended.

Outside, fog rolled in the light of the lamppost, as though trying to take shape. That was the only thing you could see. The night around it was black, and its sound constant, like the hum of a refrigerator. Crickets, leaves, wind. The quiet inside felt suspect, gave the impression that the dolls on the shelves, standing there with their eyes open, might come to life at any moment.

Now I had no peace in that house.

Every afternoon, when the fog enveloped us and Porfirio left, I felt as if my mother and I were trapped. As if something had merged with the fog outside. Rebeca, trying to slip in through the cracks. As if it was her, and not Old Viruñas or the creaky wood, causing the unexplained sounds.

I had trouble falling asleep. I would lie there in the dark and focus on the dolls, waiting for them to blink or turn their heads. Focus on the closet door, on the fog around the lamppost outside, on the horses' hooves and their neighing, on the leaves swirling, on the wind, sometimes a gentle whisper and other times a howling gale that rattled the doors and windows, on the silence of the house suddenly broken by a creak from the ceiling, a moan in the pipes like someone dying, a breeze faintly blowing through the walls.

When I finally dropped off, it was into a light sleep, one polluted by external perceptions. Shadows, lights, sounds, the weight of the covers on my body, the cold of the sheets, the faint scent of horses and the mildew smell of the pillow.

My breath would catch when I thought I saw the dolls talking among themselves or a gnarly fingernail, a skeletal finger, an arm with bulging veins reaching through the joints in the ceiling, stretching its hand out to me.

That was when I'd realize I was dreaming, and wake up terrified. I didn't fall really and truly asleep until I saw the headlights, heard the motor of the Renault 12 coming down the driveway.

One night, the headlights and sound of the motor enveloped me, but instead of letting myself go to sleep—perhaps because I sensed that the car sounded different, like it was idling—I opened my eyes. In the hallway: people, movement. I got up and opened the door.

Porfirio and my father were in the hall, the front door open. That explained the white beam of headlights streaming in, and the engine was indeed on, the motor idling. Porfirio, in a poncho, hat, and rubber boots, was opening and closing drawers at the cabinet by the door. My father was walking down the hall, a flashlight in his hand.

"What's going on?"

They both looked at me; my father said the power had gone out.

"Where's mamá?"

"Go back to bed."

Porfirio found the spare batteries he was looking for in one of the drawers, held them up to show my father.

"In case the ones in the flashlight die."

He slipped them into his pants pocket and I saw the machete in its leather sheath, hanging from his waist.

"Where is my mother?!" I asked, anguished.

As though I'd conjured her, mamá emerged from the bedroom in a thick wool sweater, her purse over one shoulder.

"You heard your father. Go to bed."

"What's going on?"

"They found a car in the abyss, an old car."

"Rebeca's?"

"Nobody knows." Her words sounded muddled, like tía Amelia when she was drunk. "The tow truck just got there."

"I want to go with you."

"No."

I looked at papá: "Please."

"Anita will stay here and look after you."

He came and gave me a hug.

"Everything is going to be fine. There's nothing to worry about."

He kissed my forehead and walked with my mother to the door.

"Don't leave me," I begged.

Before closing the door, Porfirio looked at me with pity.

The hallway was all dark. I walked into the bedroom and closed the door. Turned on the light: nothing. Outside, the car drove off, up the driveway and onto the unpaved road.

It had been a sunny day. The afternoon so warm my mother and I didn't even have to put on our sweaters, and I'd gone to bed barefoot, wearing only light, short-sleeve pajamas.

Now, in the night, I felt the cold in the air, sharp as it entered my nostrils, pricked the bottom of my feet.

Through the giant window I could see the garden, the lamppost, the fence, the canyon black as a lake.

It was a clear night, clearer than any I'd seen. Everything was silent. The trees and the horses. All of it perfectly still. The mountains in the distance, shining like fevered eyes.

I got into bed face-up, pulled the covers to my neck, and promised myself I'd think only of lovely things: the flowers in the garden, cornflowers and calla lilies, hummingbirds and robins, an orange butterfly that decided to land on my finger and sat there serenely as I observed it; our life in Cali before the fights and before Gonzalo; our apartment, the jungle down on the first floor, a pretend jungle that wasn't scary, and the stairs that were really just stairs.

I closed my eyes and a cliff appeared before me. I opened them and it was still there. The real cliff, and at the bottom, buried in the vegetation, a green car with broken windows. Rebeca in the driver's seat. The prettiest corpse ever, in an elegant white dress, her long fingers still gripping the wheel, her blonde hair, blue eyes, and skin all intact, as though no years had gone by and the car had just landed down there gracefully.

In order to stop seeing it, in order to stop thinking about her, I began counting seconds out loud—one one thousand, two one thousand, three one thousand—to stop time from stretching, to know how long it really was—four one thousand, five one thousand, six one thousand ...

I awoke face-up, the covers pulled up to my neck, just the way I'd gone to sleep, feeling like I hadn't slept for more than an instant. On the floor by the big window, a patch of light. The sun was high above the mountains, a radiant morning. The sky and earth like they'd gotten a coat of varnish.

I went into the bathroom and washed my face. Poked my head into the main bedroom. Mamá wasn't there. I went downstairs. She was at the kitchen counter, drinking coffee, in jeans and a T-shirt, with wool socks and wet hair.

"Was it Rebeca's car?"

"Good morning."

"Was it?"

"Claudia, say good morning."

"Good morning."

My mother blew on her coffee and set the cup on the counter.

"Just when everyone had forgotten all about her, when no one was looking for her, voila!"

"So it was."

"Can you believe it?"

"Was she in the car?"

She nodded yes.

"Did you see her?"

"Her bones."

A group of campesinos, she told me, had been clearing a path through the undergrowth and hit something so hard it made sparks fly from their machetes: the Studebaker, so covered in vegetation it was invisible even right there in front of them.

"Give me a description."

"The metal all crumpled, windscreens gone, rusty in some spots."

"Of Rebeca, I mean."

"Ah."

Mamá picked up her cup and turned to the window. Sparse and wispy in the blue sky, the clouds like shavings someone had forgotten to sweep up.

"She must have died instantly."

"But what did she look like?"

"Nothing but bones, I told you."

She became absent, gazing out at the scenery, and I could get nothing more out of her.

After lunch, my mother poured her first whisky, and I stuck to her like glue. She started in the fireplace room. After the second, she moved to the living room and, while she drank, I finished the jigsaw.

I was admiring the puzzle—appreciating the details, the tiny yellow flowers in the field, the soft light on the pond, the shadows on the windmill—when Porfirio came in to close the giant windows and light the fire. Mamá and I went upstairs for our sweaters.

Back downstairs, she poured another whisky then started making dinner. The fireplace was blazing. Porfirio said goodbye and I sat in the dining room with Paulina. Mamá served dinner. Cream of tomato soup and matchstick potatoes. I tried to get her to tell me more. Whether Rebeca's skull had hair on it, whether there were still any shreds of her white dress, whether they called the family, whether my mother saw or spoke to them, whether Mariú was sad, whether she cried, whether her eyes changed color.

"That's enough, Claudia."

"Why?"

"Because it terrifies you, and then you're afraid to go to bed."

"I promise I'll go to bed the second papá gets back."

"No. He's going to be late tonight, he has to wait on an order."

She had a couple bites of soup and went for her fourth whisky. We sat on the sofa in the fireplace room, her drinking slowly, just as she had all afternoon, and me, watching her out of the corner of my eye.

I don't remember how or when I got to bed. Maybe I was so tired, after several bad nights, that I fell asleep on the sofa and my mother carried me in. But I know I woke up in the girls' room.

It was the dead of night and something didn't add up. It was as if objects had been moved around, the furniture rearranged, or the amount of space had somehow changed. Or as if while I was asleep I'd been moved into a different room that was trying to pass for the girls' room.

I tried to sit up and couldn't. Tried calling for my mother and couldn't do that either. Tried to scream; no use. I focused all of my energy on my right-hand pinky and was able to move it. Relieved, I woke up.

Looking around the room, I sensed right away that it was slightly different. I tried to move but it was no use. Kept trying and finally managed to turn my head, only to wake up in a fake room. This happened several times, until I saw that a skeletal hand had grabbed my wrist.

The hand, I realized, had led me from the real room to the other side of the house. The side where she lived. The side you could sense at night, when the fog enveloped us. The hidden world where those inexplicable sounds were produced.

Then I woke up for real.

The fog was so thick that the lamppost looked farther away. A dim sun in a polluted atmosphere. You couldn't even see the fence. Suddenly I glimpsed something white a few meters below the light, something denser than fog.

I sat up in bed. A rag, a piece of cloth. I looked at my hands and was able to move them. Paulina was sleeping in the bed across from mine, as she did every night. The dolls on the shelves, their eyes open wide, looked as monstrous as ever. I was awake in the actual room, and outside that thing was flapping in the strong wind; for a minute the fog thinned.

The thing outside was a human, in a white dress.

"Mamá!"

I got up and ran to the main bedroom. My back was sweaty, my feet freezing. The bed was unmade, the giant window open, the gauze curtains blowing.

I checked the balcony, the bathroom, and the closet. Checked the other rooms and the second bathroom. Calling for her, I went downstairs. My mother wasn't in the living room, the dining room, or the kitchen, where an empty bottle of whisky sat on the counter. She wasn't in the study or the fireplace room either. I went toward the terrace, opened the sliding door.

"Mamá ..."

It was impossible to see.

"Mamá!"

I went outside. The cold wind blew my hair up and gave me goosebumps. I wanted to fall down and burst into tears. Wanted to stop looking for her. Wanted her to jump off the cliff and never come back. Wanted to be alone with my father and drown with him in the sea of his silence. But I kept searching, and when I was sure my mother wasn't on the terrace, I came back inside.

I went upstairs and opened the door to the garden, fear pounding in my chest. The fog, which looked thick in the light of the front door, blew as fast as the wind, which whipped through the trees and howled furiously like a ghost as it entered the canyon.

I walked down the driveway to the end of the house, the wind in my face, and continued through the grass. Making my way farther, objects materialized: the lamppost, the flimsy fence, incapable of restraining a thing, and the shape of the human, feet on the ground, white dress flapping. And masses of hair, and the same white robe as my mother.

"Mamá."

I was afraid it was Rebeca and not her.

"Mamá?"

The back exactly like mamá's, the front that of a dead woman.

"Namesake," I called, softly.

She turned. It was her. Healthy, whole.

"What are you doing?"

"I just came out for a walk."

In the middle of the night, barefoot and in pajamas, like Natalie Wood.

"I'd never been over to this side of the property."

A very steep cliff.

"It's been so long since the two of us went for a walk, hasn't it?"

Her voice came out crooked, drunken. She held a glass in her hand. Stumbled. I took a step forward and grabbed her forearm, so thin my hand could almost encircle it: Karen Carpenter.

"Let's go back to the house, mamá."

"We'll go out tomorrow, the two of us. I promise."

The cliff was behind her, two steps back. Though you couldn't see it for the fog, it was there, vast as the one Princess Grace drove off. I felt its power, the thread at the bottom of it, tugging her.

"Her little bones were all broken to pieces."

"Rebeca's?"

"She sure knew how to do it right."

Then I saw it in her eyes. The abyss inside her, just like it was in all of the dead women, in Gloria Inés, a bottomless pit that nothing could fill.

"This is the perfect place to disappear."

"Let's go," I said, and pulled her.

My mother allowed herself to be led over the grass and up the driveway, back to the house.

Once inside, I took her glass and set it on the cabinet by the door. She grabbed it and downed what was left. I closed the door, and the wind, the howling, and the force stayed outside. We went to the main bedroom, mamá docile and unsteady, me making sure she didn't fall. I sat her down on the bed, took off her robe and wet socks, and helped her lie down.

She closed her eyes. Her hair was windswept and she wore a calm expression, like a stubborn child overcome by sheer exhaustion. She reeked of whisky. A dead wood smell. I breathed it and held it. I wanted to save her smell inside the way my father had saved his tía Mona's talcum-powder smell. My mother's scent, so I'd never forget. I stroked her forehead, then her hair. Untangled it with my fingers until it was straight and shiny. I kissed her forehead and lay down beside her. She opened her eyes.

"Your father's still not home?"

"No."

"It's very late."

She closed her eyes and seemed to fall asleep instantly. Laying there with mine open, I pictured my father in an accident, out on the road. My father, at the bottom of the cliff, the monster inside him asleep forevermore, his mother by his side, happy to see him at last. His mother as a little girl, and him as an old man. I cried with no tears. So tired my eyes were closing. I held my mother's wrist tight, so she couldn't go anyplace, so I'd know if she tried to get up and could keep her here with me, on this side of the house.

When I awoke the following morning it was light out and I was in the girls' room. I went to the main bedroom. Empty. Went downstairs. My mother was in the kitchen making breakfast, my father in the dining room.

"You came back!"

I hugged him.

"You don't remember me taking you to bed?"

"No."

"You were talking."

"What did I say?"

"You asked how come I'd taken so long."

"I did?"

"And I told you the delivery had been delayed."

My mother served us eggs and arepas. My father and I cleaned our plates, and she drank three glasses of water, took two bites of her arepa, and pushed her eggs around without eating them.

"Not hungry?" papá asked.

"I have a headache."

She left her food and went upstairs to bathe. He opened the newspaper.

"Let's go back to Cali," I said.

"Aren't you having a nice time here?"

"It's my birthday in three days and I don't want to be here."

"Why not?"

"This place is bad."

"Bad how?"

"There are cliffs."

"Beautiful ones."

"I don't want you and mamá to die."

He lowered the paper.

"Come here."

He folded it and set it on the table, and I sat on his lap.

"You're afraid we're going to die?"

"You'll have an accident like Rebeca, and mamá will jump."

"I drive very carefully, I've told you that a thousand times, and your mother is not going to jump."

"How do you know?"

"A mother wouldn't leave her daughter. You said so yourself."

"Paulina said that."

"Fine, Paulina then."

"Gloria Inés left her children."

"She fell over the balcony. Your mother is not going to fall. Haven't you seen the railings and windows everywhere?"

"Princes Grace and Natalie Wood had children too."

"Those stories really upset you."

"Please, let's leave this house."

"Gloria Inés was ill."

"Mamá is too."

My father laughed.

"Your mother has a headache."

"She's been sick since Cali."

"She doesn't have rhinitis anymore and there are no guayacanes here."

"You're never here, you don't know."

"What don't I know?"

"Last night she got drunk. She went out in her socks and walked across the grass all the way to the fence by the cliff. If I hadn't been there, she might have jumped. She told me it was the perfect place to disappear."

"She was very upset by the whole Rebeca thing too." He kissed my forehead. "But can't you see how much better she's gotten since we've been here? She doesn't need allergy medicine anymore."

"Now she needs whisky."

He laughed again.

"One little whisky from time to time never hurt anybody."

My father and I went in the private waterfall, and I spent the rest of the morning playing in the girls' room. At lunchtime we grilled and ate out on the terrace and my father asked if we wanted to go for a walk.

"You two go," my mother said.

"I'm staying with her," I said.

We went inside and mamá poured herself a whisky. He asked if it wasn't too early for a drink.

"You want one?" she responded.

He said no and suggested we play parcheesi. I glanced at my mother. Whisky in hand, she looked at us, searching for an excuse.

"I want to read that magazine you brought me," she told my father.

Vanidades. On the cover, a woman in a leopard-print bodysuit. She picked up the magazine and went into the fireplace room.

My father and I played parcheesi in the dining room. A beetle kept climbing up the window, slipping down, and starting over, flapping its wings with a metallic buzz. I got two pieces home. It was looking like I was about to win, since my father had two in jail, but he rolled three doubles in a row, got two home, and from then on was unstoppable. We played another round and he beat me again.

Porfirio came to close the giant windows and light the fire. My mother told us it was getting cold and we went upstairs. They went into the main bedroom. Me to the girls' room, where I took a sweater out of the closet, and then got Paulina—so pretty and elegant in her green velvet dress—and brushed her hair.

My mother dished out the pasta and sat down across from my father. I sat at the head of the table.

"Where's Paulina?" she asked. "Isn't she going to eat with us tonight?"

"Paulina's gone."

"What do you mean?"

"She jumped off the cliff."

My parents looked bewildered.

"Did you drop her?" mamá asked.

I'd felt nothing at the edge of the precipice, not even dizzy. The sky was white, the mountains black, thick fog covered the canyon.

"No," I replied. "She jumped."

First Paulina sat on the fence, like the kids that sat on the wall above the lions' moat. Calm, as though just taking in the scenery.

"What are you saying, Claudia?"

She was up in the air, with me holding her by the arm.

"That she committed suicide."

I watched her fall. First, straight down. Then she tilted to one side and a shoe fell off.

"Did you throw her?"

"She threw herself."

Paulina, in the air. Head over heels, little feet pointing up, head down, long hair fanned out, flapping like wings.

"Over the cliff?"

"Yes, over the cliff."

I watched her enter the canyon fog and disappear into the thick white.

"Why?" my mother asked.

My father was staring at me.

"Because she didn't want to go on living anymore."

Unsure what to say, they stared at me.

"Some people just want to die," I added.

The beetle that had been attempting to climb up the window was now on the ground, upside down and motionless, its tiny legs sticking up.

"Claudia," she asked, "do you want to die?"

My response: a gesture that meant nothing.

PART FOUR

THE FOLLOWING MORNING, very early, we packed up our suitcases and carried them out to the car. Porfirio and Anita were taken aback when they realized we were leaving before planned. They both came out to open the big gate.

I waved goodbye from the car until they disappeared from view. Then I turned around and settled on the back seat which, without Paulina, felt as big as a soccer field.

The unpaved road seemed just as dark and sinister as it had to me on arrival, but not as long. It only took a few minutes to reach the main road. And as soon as we had descended a few meters, the day cleared and we could see the blue sky and amazing sun. Up at that house, I thought, we'd been living inside clouds.

We drove in silence. Patches of forest, roadside restaurants, and country houses, until we got to Cerezo's Curve. We rocked, and again I missed Paulina, who would have fallen on her side. When we came out of the curve, the enormous precipice appeared, straight ahead of us, and behind it, in the distance, Cali splayed in the valley.

My father drove us to the apartment, helped us take the suitcases up, and then went to the supermarket. My mother and I unpacked, put away our clothes and my toys, and went down to survey the jungle.

She turned around, silent, examining everything, and I did the same. Lucila approached.

"I gave them the urea Señor Jorge brought two weeks ago."

"I can tell," mamá said, smiling, but it was only so Lucila wouldn't feel bad.

In reality the plants looked sad, their leaves droopy and yellowing. Lucila said she had to prepare lunch and went back to the kitchen. My mother carried on with her inspection, walking among the plants, gazing at each one. Finally she went to the forest behind the three-seater sofa and began pinching dry leaves off the ficus.

All my dead, I thought. If my father's dead resided in his silence and my mother's dead were the plants in the jungle, mine were the leaves about to fall. My grandmother as a girl, my bitter grandfather, tía Mona, my grandfather the bear, my worm-and-cobra grandmother, the women in those magazines, Gloria Inés, Paulina ...

Outside, the guayacanes had lost their leaves. All that was left were bare branches, a few wilted flowers. The ground was littered with those that had fallen off, a carpet of blossoms. Once pink, now faded, brown and dirty.

"Are they going to die?"

"Who?"

"The guayacanes."

"No, namesake," my mother said. "They always come back."

Suddenly I felt a gentle touch on my shoulder and jumped, startled. Turning, I saw one of the palm trees, its finger-fronds reaching out to me.

"Hello," I said back.

My father came home at lunchtime and we sat down at the table. Though they didn't say so, my parents, like me, must have felt Paulina's absence, the empty chair. Serving me, my mother asked if I wanted to go to the bouncy trampoline.

"Yeah!"

"Papá spoke to your tía; she's going to take you."

"For your birthday," he said.

I climbed into the front seat of my aunt's Renault 6, we hugged.

On the way there, she plied me with questions. What was the house like, how did the trip go, what did I think of it, how did I feel? I told her fine, fine, fine, and fine. She took her eyes off the road and looked at me, smiling.

The trampoline was under a big top, a circus tent in a dusty lot; it had a metallic base and a huge black sheet of rubber and looked like a giant's cot. I jumped for several tickets in a row, cautious to begin with, and then bouncing higher and higher.

My feet drove down into the rubber and I sprang up, flying toward the far-off top of the multicolored tent. The luscious sensation in my tummy, a little ball of joy, flowed through me, exploding at my navel and traveling all the way to my fingertips, all the way to my windswept hair. Then I looked down and got vertigo. Tía Amelia, the man in charge of turn-keeping, the metal tables, the booth—all of it so tiny. The world, smashed on the ground, and me, suspended in the air, like I'd gone over a cliff and was going to die like poor Paulina. The nausea of that fear gathered at my center, but my feet returned to the rubber, up I flew, and again the deliciousness exploded.

All of a sudden I noticed my aunt looking up, hands megaphoned around her mouth. Her shouting traversed the invisible layers of the worlds separating us and I heard her voice:

"Claudiaaaaaaaa!"

And the turn-keeper:

"Your time is uuuuup!"

I got off the trampoline, returned to solid ground.

"It's time for a snack," my tía said.

It was like landing on a different planet. I was red and flustered, my hair soaked with sweat. There wasn't even a hint of a breeze and it felt like all of Cali's sweltering heat had amassed under the big top. We bought salty-sweet popcorn and two Castalias, and sat down. I took a sip of soda and my brain froze.

"Happy almost-birthday," my aunt said.

"Thank you."

I wiped my mouth with my hand. She lit a cigarette.

"So you had a good time in the mountains."

"Yes."

I took a handful of popcorn.

"And Paulina?" she asked.

My aunt had given her to me, and now she was gone. What could I say? Luckily I was chewing and had an excuse not to talk.

"Your father told me you lost her."

"Will you forgive me?"

"I'm not scolding you, sweetheart. I just want to know what happened."

She exhaled a stream of smoke; it spiraled up.

"I know she was your favorite dolly."

"Yes."

"So?"

"She jumped off the cliff."

"All by her lonesome?"

I nodded and grabbed more popcorn. We sat in silence. My tía smoking, me eating. When she finished smoking she tossed the butt on the ground and crushed it under a shoe.

"Paulina leapt off the cliff, all by herself ..."

I tried to smile so she wouldn't see how I really felt, but my face scrunched up. She put her arm around me.

"You weren't happy at that house, were you?"

I shook my head no.

"Why not?"

A tear escaped.

"I was scared."

I wiped it away.

"Of what?"

"Old Viruñas."

"Someone talked to you about Old Viruñas?"

"The caretaker."

"When your father and I were little, the cook at the country house used to scare us with stories of Old Viruñas. If we lost something, our pencil or notebook, she'd say Old Viruñas had taken it. I was always scared to death, but deep down I knew it was made up. You're very intelligent, Claudia. Do you really think Old Viruñas exists?"

"The fog scared me too."

"Yes, it's very mysterious."

"And the house, it was all weird, you walked in on the upstairs and the living room was on the bottom."

"Your father said the house was very pretty."

"A lady disappeared there."

"You were scared of Rebeca O'Brien?"

"I thought she was going to appear."

"You were afraid of a ghost."

"And that my parents would disappear like she did."

"Why would they disappear?"

"Papá could have an accident on the road."

"True, that's very scary."

"The abyss is very scary."

"Terrifying."

"Yes."

"What about your mother?"

"What about my mother?"

"Why were you afraid she might disappear?"

I pretended like I didn't know.

"She didn't do any driving while you were there."

"No."

"Well then?"

"She could have fallen."

"Fallen how?"

"Like Gloria Inés."

"Gloria Inés was up on a bench."

"She could have jumped."

"Why would she jump?"

I remained silent. Ate. Drank my soda. My tía kept at it:

"Why?"

"Because she's sick."

"With rhinitis?"

I shook my head.

"What do you mean, sick?"

"Like Gloria Inés."

"She told you that?"

"No."

"Who said so?"

"Nobody, but I know."

"What about you?"

"What about me?"

"Did you want to jump?"

I looked at her.

"No."

"You just wanted to come back to Cali."

"And I wanted it to be like it was before Gonzalo."

Now it was my aunt's face that scrunched up. We hugged and cried together.

That night my mother came to my room with me without me even asking. I got into bed. She turned out the nightstand lamp and sat down on my bed.

"I know I haven't been the best mother."

I felt the urge to console her, tell her that it wasn't true, say she was the best mother in the world, but it had done me good to cry on tía Amelia's bosom that day, to jump for hours on the trampoline, to stuff myself with popcorn and soda, and I kept quiet.

"When sadness gets into my body, I try to make it go, I swear I do."

She was a silhouette in the dark; I couldn't see her expression.

"You're the most important thing to me, Claudia. Even though sometimes sadness gets the best of me, you're the only truly important thing. Do you know that?"

I stayed quiet.

"I promise I'm going to try my best, I'm going to fight harder and not let it come back again."

A tear spilled silently from my eye, but I was lying still and don't think she noticed.

"REBECA'S WAKE IS this afternoon," my mother said at breakfast. "Your father and I think it would be good if you came with us."

I looked at him and he smiled.

"Would you like that?" she asked.

"Yeah!"

"I talked to Mariú last night and she said the girls are going to be there. I know you wanted to meet them."

I bathed slowly. Shampooed my hair, used conditioner. Washed my bellybutton with soap, and behind my ears, and the folds of my arms and legs. Then I put on my blue party pants, white button-down shirt, and suede yellow-striped Adidas. I straightened my bangs with my mother's hair dryer and tied a ribbon the same color as my pants in my hair. Took out my Fresita strawberry lip gloss, which had lain abandoned in my nightstand drawer for months. The smell filled my room when I opened it, and I smeared some on my lips.

My father had put on a jacket and tie. My mother, so beautiful, was in a black knee-length dress, her hair down, lips painted red.

The wake was at the house that Fernando Ceballos built for Rebeca when they got married. It was near tía Amelia's apartment, on a quiet block that, on this occasion, had a long line of parked cars outside.

It was a two-story flat-roofed house with black columns out front and a curved wall of orange tile on the second floor. There was a big garage door on the first floor, and another smaller door for people. The main entrance was upstairs. We walked up a staircase sloped as gently as a ramp. The second we rang, the door opened, as if they'd been waiting for us.

A smiling man, the same age as my father, welcomed us. He was blond, suntanned, and had wrinkles and blue eyes that made me think of my mother's description of Patrick: two giant gemstones in the desert. Was that him? Excited, I glanced at mamá. She smiled.

"Please, follow me," the man said.

He gestured to a spiral staircase leading down to a large hall where all the guests were gathered. A giant window at the back went from the bottom of the first floor to the top of the second, like our living room, and overlooked the river, the trees, the garden. On the second floor, where we were, hallways went off to both sides, with a series of closed doors.

The man said he was off to buy ice, because at an Irish wake you needed plenty for the whisky, and walked out, closing the door.

"That's Michael," mamá said quietly, "the oldest one."

My father straightened his tie.

On the ground floor, people were everywhere, inside and out—the parlor, the living room, the dining room, the veranda, by the pool, and in the garden bordering the river, which had rocks, rain trees, grass, and plants that looked wild even though they weren't. There were people of all ages, two waiters, several maids in the kitchen, and a priest in a black cassock with a purple sash.

My attention was drawn to an old lady so white it was hard to tell her forehead from her hair. She had the clearest blue eyes I'd ever seen and was dressed to the nines, all in linen. She looked like something from another world. More extraterrestrial than foreign, a being from a distant galaxy, one where there was no sunlight. She sat in the living room, in an armchair, an aluminum walker before her. This woman was never alone, not for a second. I later learned she was Rebeca's mother. The father had died years ago and she was the only person at the whole event who was sad.

It was easy to tell the O'Briens from the guests. Even though some were blonder, whiter, or taller than others, they all had the same family traits: the height, eyes, and skin color, the angular, sculpted features. They talked, drank, and laughed, and nobody scolded the children shouting and running around. It was more like a party than a wake.

I recognized Mariú, Liliana, and the girls immediately from the photos. The husbands too, but they didn't interest me. Mariú was in black trousers and a white blouse and had her hair down. She smiled when she saw my mother. They kissed and hugged, and my mother said sweet, loving things to her.

Looking at me, Mariú asked, "Is this Claudia?"

"This is Claudia."

Mariú crouched down to my height. She had gray eyes with light and dark flecks, and as she gazed at me, attentive and up close, I felt her beauty wash over me.

"Isn't she pretty," said the prettiest one of all.

She straightened up. My mother thanked her for the phony compliment and Mariú looked around.

"Mine are over there."

The older girl, my age, was conversing with a group of adults in grown-up fashion, amid all the rattan out on the veranda. The other two, one hers and the other Liliana's, were leaping in the garden, arm in arm. All three had French braids and wore identical white dresses, embroidered down the front, with puffy sleeves and a bow at the back.

"Just beautiful," said my mother, truly admiring. "Those dresses look like sugar." She placed a hand on my shoulder. "This one, on the other hand, refuses to wear anything but pants. It's a miracle she wore elegant ones today, though with tennis shoes, as you can see."

Maríu looked at my suede Adidas with the yellow stripes.

"I'd wear tennies all the time if I could."

"Isn't that the truth," said mamá.

Mariú winked at me.

"Those are sensational."

Liliana walked over. Greeted us kindly, distantly. She was shorter and fuller than her sister, and had dimples on both sides of her mouth. My father, who'd lagged behind, caught up, and María and Liliana turned to him.

I spotted two other men who had to have been Rebeca's brothers. They wore jackets and ties, were as smooth as the man who'd opened the door, and of a similar age—not quite old men yet—suntanned, with athletic builds. I wondered if one of them was Patrick. My mother showed no sign of being flustered.

Standing beside my father, she was telling a group of people how the locals had found Rebeca's car buried in the vegetation. A waiter passed offering whisky, and she debated. In the end she declined. My father took one though.

Then I saw him. Michael, the eldest, walked in through a side door with two bags of ice, and behind him, with a couple of bottles of whisky—him. It had to be Patrick. An O'Brien to the letter. Tall and strong, but younger than the other ones and not dressed up in the slightest. He wasn't wearing a jacket or tie, had his shirtsleeves rolled up, and his hair looked like it had never seen a brush in its life.

Michael and Patrick walked into the kitchen. My mother didn't see them. The group's eyes were all on her as she recounted the moment when the car, having been hauled up by the tow truck's crane— crushed, broken, rusty, but still green—emerged from the precipice.

Michael and Patrick came back to the living room. Maybe it was the swinging doors that made mamá look over. She was stunned, left her words hanging in the air, and in my own exploding heart I could feel the commotion inside hers. Someone asked a question and my mother returned, answering as best she could.

Patrick, who still hadn't seen my mother, took a whisky from a waiter's tray. A woman walked over to him. Broad-hipped, dark-skinned, her curly hair wild. She wore sandals and a flowery dress, held a baby in one arm and led a small child by the hand. After saying something to Patrick, they laughed, and he took the baby. She followed, guiding the other child by the hand, to the stairs. This was his family. The children—I later learned there were three—had their mother's dark skin and their father's light eyes.

Patrick, after a sip of whisky, scanned the room and discovered my mother. From afar, with no intention of going over, he smiled. She smiled too. He drank his whisky and she filled her chest with air. My father, silent, was all eyes.

At the back of the house was a study with its door open. The casket lay on a table, covered by a cloth, between two bouquets of white roses. I had never seen one up close or in person, especially not with a corpse inside.

No one stopped me walking up to it.

The study looked like a flower shop. The casket was sealed, and small and white, a box for a baby. Rebeca was in there. A full-grown woman in that tiny space. Just her bones. Little bones broken to pieces, like my mother said. I pictured them worn, shattered, their insides visible, dark, smelly, and at the top end her empty skull, a skull with no glory, like any other dead body.

On the back wall was a bookcase, in the center a big black-and-white photo. The bust of a woman looking off to one side with a mischievous smile. Rebeca O'Brien, definitely. She had a high brow, and her hair was in a low bun. Her dress, what you could see of it, was sleeveless and cinched at the waist. She looked more like Mariú than Liliana. It was Mariú, with the elegance of the woman in the armchair, the eyes of her brothers, and Liliana's dimples.

"Thank goodness they found you," I said, hardly moving my lips.

A gray-haired old man walked into the study. Fernando Ceballos, I recognized him instantly. Strong and healthy. He stood by my side and looked down at me, unkindly, as though wondering: who on earth is *this*? Behind him came the priest with his purple sash, the woman with the walker, Mariú, Liliana, Rebeca's brothers, the nieces and nephews, and the rest of the family and guests. In all the commotion, I slipped away.

The priest, Fernando, Michael, and the other brothers all spoke at the ceremony. The woman with the walker cried, Mariú and Liliana broke down too. Then Patrick told a joke and everybody laughed. I don't remember the speeches, just two things that Mariú said:

"Thank you for coming home, mother." And she looked at *my* mother. "And thank you, Claudia, for bringing her back to us."

The girls headed out to the garden and I trailed along after. I wandered in wide circles around them and the dozen or so other kids, looking on from the distance as they argued over the rules to a game.

"Do you want to play with us?"

"Play what?"

"Hide and seek."

"Okay."

"What's your name?"

"Claudia. What's yours?"

"Rebeca."

It was Mariú's oldest, with her French braid and sugar-dress. Golden-peach fuzz around her eyebrows and at the baby hair on the sides of her face, as though she she'd been bathed in light at birth.

"Her name is Claudia," she told the group. "She's going to play with us. And no hiding upstairs, like I said. Who's it?"

"The new girl," said a skinny boy with long legs.

"No, *you* are, dummy," Rebeca replied, defending me. "She's never been to the house."

The boy protested. He had olive-green eyes and the family features, with brown skin and curly hair. Patrick's oldest, surely. Cute, except for being such a dummy. Nobody stuck up for him, so he had to go to the wall and count.

I hid in the big hall, behind a piece of furniture. From there, I caught sight of my mother in the other room. She was conversing with some ladies who, each and every one of them, held a cup of coffee. Mamá was drinking whisky.

Patrick's son was tiptoeing over. Cold, warmer, hot, boiling. He found me! I ran for base, but his legs were so long.

"Claudia's it," he said, touching a hand to the wall before me.

But I didn't have to be it on the next round after all, because the last boy, a big kid, made it back to base and called all-safe, which meant Patrick's son was it again. I decided to hide in the garden behind some big bushes with red flowers. It was a tight spot and Rebeca was already there. I was about to go elsewhere, but she waved me in, making space for me.

"I love your pants," she whispered.

"Thank you," I whispered back.

Patrick's son finished counting and started seeking.

"I wish I could wear pants."

"You're not allowed to wear them?"

"Only when we go to the country house or stay at home."

"Don't you like dresses?"

"Not much."

"Me either. But yours is really pretty."

"Thank you."

"And your braids too."

"Thank you."

"Do they hurt your head?"

"Like crazy. My mother pulls so hard sometimes tears stream down my face."

I gave her a pitying look.

"Your mother doesn't do your hair?"

"No. The most she does is make me wear a bow," I said, showing her the one I had tied into my hair. "This one I put on myself, without her telling me to, because I wanted to look elegant. I've never been to a wake."

"Me either."

"And I've had tons of people die."

"Really?"

"All four of my grandparents and one of my father's aunts, before I was born. And just recently one of my mother's cousins, who was like a sister to her."

"And you didn't go to the wake?"

"They wouldn't take me."

We were talking very close, face-to-face, her blue eyes on mine.

"You have really good teeth," she said.

We'd both had new ones come in. But mine were in a straight line, and hers, big as paddles, were all crooked, pointy canines overlapping her other teeth.

"Thank you."

"When I'm older, I'm going to get braces."

"Nice."

"They say they hurt like crazy, worse than braids."

"Sometimes I wear braces I make out of tin foil."

"Me too."

She told me that at Irish wakes people didn't sleep, and she was going to try to stay up all night with the adults, and the following day they were taking her grandmother to the cemetery, to an ossuary, which was like a cubbyhole for bones.

"Have you ever seen one?"

"Never."

"Me either."

"I've never been to a cemetery."

"Sounds scary."

"Yeah, sounds scary."

"I'm named for my dead grandmother."

"I'm named for my mother, but she's not dead."

"Thank goodness."

We were so engaged in our conversation that we didn't realize Patrick's son had found us.

"Rebeca and Claudia are it!"

"Oh, damn," she said, and we roared with laughter.

Me and Rebeca were walking to the wall when my father, who appeared out of nowhere, grabbed my arm.

"We're leaving."

It wasn't even dark yet.

"We just started playing."

"Just a little longer," Rebeca said, supporting me.

"Pretty pleeeeeease."

"It's time, Claudia."

"Did mamá say so?"

She was the one who made those decisions.

I searched for her everywhere, among all the people. Outside, inside, sitting, standing, in living and sitting and dining rooms. The elderly lady with the walker was back in her armchair. Fernando Ceballos, in the kitchen doorway, was saying something to Mariú. Patrick's wife was walking behind a baby who was tottering exactly like a drunk. Liliana was speaking to a couple on the wicker furniture out on the veranda. In the dining room beside it, kids were playing cards.

I went back to my father. He directed his gaze toward the floor-to-ceiling window. Then I saw her. Standing apart from the little groups, with Patrick, each with a whisky in their hand.

"I have to go," I said to Rebeca.

"Such an impressive house, isn't it?"

This was my mother asking, in the car. My father, at the wheel, did not respond.

"Very," I said.

"The garden didn't used to have those huge shrubs, or the pool."

Papá, still silent.

"Though it looked smaller too, I thought. The house. It's enormous, of course. But back then I thought it was big as a convent."

Then my father spoke.

"You were totally gaga."

"Excuse me?"

I was as taken aback as she was.

"He was the only thing you had eyes for; you couldn't see anything else."

"What are you talking about, Jorge?"

Coiled tight as a slingshot, he whipped his head sideways to glare at her, enraged.

"I was never even with him," my mother said, defensively. "I'm talking about one single time, when I was a little girl and got invited to Mariú's birthday."

He turned back to face front, his monster roused.

"Are you angry?"

No response.

"The man lives in Puerto Rico. He's leaving the day after tomorrow. He's happily married, with three kids. His wife and children were all there. You and Claudia too ..."

My father remained mute. The monster, I sensed in his labored breathing, was surfacing.

Sleep did not take me fully that night, didn't submerge me in its depths, where everything is soft and detached from the world; instead it left me in a limbo, a waking sleep where I was trapped in the tiny space between my closed eyelids and my eyes.

I saw Rebeca, the granddaughter, struggling not to fall asleep at the wake. I saw Old Viruñas, in with all the people, all cagey and hunched over, moving as though he were me, in the mirror at the country house. Rebeca was nodding off and he was creeping up to her, but nobody could see him because he was on the other side of the wall. He had a huge head, with a squashed fig nose, and a dwarf body, like me in the Christmas-tree balls at Zas. Rebeca's eyes were closing, she couldn't keep them open, and I realized Old Viruñas was not me but my father the monster. He started braiding Rebeca's hair and made her cry. Her eyes were closed, not in sleep but because she was dead, and suddenly she was no longer Rebeca-the-girl but Rebeca-the-adult, her disappeared grandmother, buried in the downstairs jungle in our apartment, covered by the fallen leaves—my dead—and so small she fit in a white baby-sized box. My father-monster, when he finished braiding her hair, got smaller and smaller until he fit into a gap between her gnarled teeth, and then she wasn't disappeared-Rebeca anymore but my father's child-mother, happy because he was inside her again, in her belly.

Suddenly I was at the mountain house. It was nighttime. I was standing at the hall mirror and my reflection showed me, small and dark, in a white nightie, Paulina in my arms. We had the same French braids as the girls and our heads hurt. Fog passed before us, then enveloped us, and when it dissolved, we were on the edge of the cliff. The abyss was calling, tugging at us. I offered up Paulina, in an attempt to appease it, and though the abyss devoured her she wasn't enough; it wanted me too. Claudia, it called. Claudiaaa, howling like the wind when it tunneled through the canyon. I fought with all my might, trying to sever the thread at the bottom of the abyss, the thread that was pulling me down through the dry leaves that were my dead.

Then, unable to get me to jump so it could devour me, the abyss slipped inside me, got in through my eyes, which was both delicious and horrific, a little ball dancing in my belly and a sickening pestilent nausea that buried itself deep inside me.

Sunlight. I opened my eyes. It was daytime, and just like that time at the mountain house, it felt as if no time had passed since I closed my eyes.

It was my birthday, Independence Day. Lucila was off, so my mother made breakfast and we sat down to eat. My father refused to look at her.

"Are the eggs good?"

"Mm-hmm."

"Should I pass the salt?"

"No."

"I was thinking, we should go to the club."

"And how do we get in?" he asked flatly.

"We ask Gloria Inés's husband to sign us in. We can have lunch there, spend the afternoon at the pool. We could invite Amelia."

"Yeah!" I shouted, excited. "Let's invite tía Amelia!"

"She won't want to."

"Well, then just us three."

At the club my mother spent a little more time attempting to appease my father, but he wouldn't react, so she gave up and started behaving just like him. Refused to look at him, didn't speak to him, and walked as if her neck was paralyzed and she couldn't turn her head.

That night, at dinner, he looked at her. Mamá: no reaction, stiff neck.

The next morning, at breakfast, he spoke to her.

"Could you pass the sugar?"

Without looking at him, she slid the sugar bowl in my father's direction.

"Thank you," he said, smiling.

She carried on like that, but his monster had been placated, and by the time we finished breakfast my parents were talking to each other again and everything went back to normal.

Tía Amelia gave me a pair of blue jeans and a T-shirt for my birthday. My parents, two more outfits. When my father left for the supermarket the following day, my mother and I went up to my room to try on my new clothes.

"Were you nervous when you saw Patrick?" she asked.

We had yet to bathe and she was sitting on my bed, in her pajamas, her hair all disheveled.

"Yes. He's handsome."

"Isn't he?"

"So's his son, even though he's dumb."

"Why is he dumb?"

I didn't know what to say.

"Maybe that means you actually liked him?"

"Nooo!" I was indignant.

She laughed.

"Do you still like Patrick?"

Now she was the one who didn't know what to say.

"I shouldn't have had a drink," she said. And then, "Try on those pants, namesake, get going."

Her feet must have touched something under my bed, because she bent over to look and found the portrait, the one I'd made of her in art class. She pulled it out. The surprise I'd wanted to give her on her birthday, when she had rhinitis and didn't even look at her gift. Now she stared it, astonished.

"This is amazing."

It was square. A profile, with a mustard-yellow background the same shade as our Renault 12, because the color looked good on her and she'd requested it. In the photo I'd copied it from she was wearing a blue shirt. In the painting I'd made it burgundy, same as her lips. Her nose was straight and triangular and her hair down. I'd worked hard to make it look real, not just a blob but a mass of individual, chocolate-colored strands.

"How come we didn't hang this up, huh?"

I shrugged.

"Oh, Claudia, please forgive me."

She stood. Held it up against the wall in my room. I told her it would go better in the study, with the other family portraits.

"You're right."

We went to get the hammer and nails. After holding it up one place and another, we decided to put it next to my birth photo. An oil painting of my mother, unframed, rendered by my young hand.

School was starting in a few days. My mother and I went shopping to buy my uniforms. The store was narrow, crammed with metal racks so full of clothes it was hard to walk. María del Carmen and her mother came in after us.

While our mothers talked, María del Carmen and I went out to the forecourt. She was peeling. She told me about her vacation in San Andrés and I told her about mine at the house of a lady who disappeared. She opened her eyes wide. I told her she'd appeared at the bottom of an abyss, and about the bones, and the wake, and the little white casket. Her eyes opened wider. Then we realized that the little wall in the forecourt could be a terrifying cliff, and walked back and forth on it, balancing so as not to fall in.

"I'd like to get a job," my mother said that night as we were eating empanadas.

My father and I stared at her in shock.

"María del Carmen's mother says they're hiring at La Pinacoteca."

"What's that?" I asked.

"A furniture store."

"What would your job be?"

"Saleswoman. They're not looking for people with experience, they want housewives. María del Carmen's mother worked there this summer while María del Carmen was at gymnastics."

She could do three backwards somersaults in a row.

"I want to do gymnastics!"

"I could request weekday shifts, work in the mornings while Claudia is at school. Saturdays she could go with you to the supermarket."

"You wouldn't take me to gymnastics?"

"There'd be no need to."

"But I want to."

"We can discuss that another time, Claudia. Right now we're talking about my job."

We looked at my father.

"I don't understand why you want to work."

My father didn't understand, but he didn't put up a fight. School vacation ended, I went back to school, and my mother started her job.

She got up early, had breakfast with us in her

pajamas, and then went upstairs to decide what to wear. After I got ready, with my hair combed and my uniform on, I helped her. We'd lay all her clothes out on the bed, place heels on the floor under them, take her jewelry out of its boxes.

"The lapis lazuli necklace goes better," I might say.

Or: "Those heels don't match at all."

Lucila would shout up the stairs that I was going to be late for school. Then I'd kiss my mother and run down.

La Pinacoteca was on Eighth Avenue in a two-story building that was once a family residence. Its windows were now showcases with expensive rattan merchandise. I had only seen it from the outside, going by in the car, but I could picture mamá inside, so pretty in whatever clothes we'd picked out that customers were besotted with my mother instead of the furniture and decor she was trying to sell them.

She always got home before me and I'd come back to find her happy, still wearing her makeup, still in her nice clothes, full of stories. Mamá talked and talked. She told me about the customers, about foreigners who couldn't speak Spanish, her botched English, the trouble she had working out discounts since she was bad at math and using a calculator, what she'd managed to sell, and the exorbitant prices they charged for everything in the store.

At night, over dinner, she'd repeat the stories so my father could hear them too and we'd laugh again.

One Friday when I got home from school, I couldn't find her. I searched the whole downstairs, and then the upstairs—her room, my room, the study, the bathroom ...

"Lucila, where's my mother?" I shouted down from the hallway railing.

She emerged from the kitchen.

"She called to say she'd be a little late today."

Lucila was holding a plate, my lunch already served.

"Come and eat, Miss Claudia."

She carried it to the dining room and went back into the kitchen. I went downstairs and sat. Even though it was full of plants, the apartment felt empty and too big. The jungle had come back to life, its leaves as green as if my mother had just shined them. Then I heard the tinkling of keys and of her, the door opening, her heels. I got up and ran to her.

"Hi, mamá."

"Look," she said, pulling out her wallet.

"That's a ton of money!"

"It's not that much," she laughed, "but it's my first paycheck."

That afternoon she took me to Sears. First we went to the toy section, where there was a doll I liked that reminded me of Paulina. Then in the clothes section, they had some denim overalls and a red T-shirt I liked. I couldn't make up my mind which I wanted and she bought them both for me.

We walked over to Dari. After paying, we went out to the tables, me holding my ice cream. We sat. The doll had reddish-brown hair, though not as much of it as Paulina, and blue eyes, but cheap ones, her eyelids didn't close and the lashes were painted onto her skin.

"They're dead," I said.

"Who?"

"Her eyes, look."

My mother was gazing at Zas. Between the distance, the shadows, and the lighting, you couldn't see in the window. Two cars were parked on the street, and between them, the leaves of a tree trembled in the wind. The door opened and a man came out. He wasn't holding a shopping bag and didn't walk away; he was just getting some air. A sales clerk. He was dressed like Gonzalo, a light shirt and black pants, tight on his butt.

"Mamá, thank you for the presents."

She turned to me, slowly.

"I love them." I smiled at her.

It wasn't long before my mother came home late again, still dressed up, still made up, her hair and accessories perfect, but zero enthusiasm.

"I'm beat."

I was eating lunch.

"Did you have a hard day?"

She flopped into a chair.

"Look what time it is. I almost didn't even get out. My feet ache from all the standing."

She took off her heels.

"Poor mamá."

"There were these three Japanese tourists. I couldn't understand a word they said. Showed them all our merchandise. Ran up and down the store three times, one side to the other, first floor, second floor. And what do you think they bought?"

"What?"

"The cheapest picture frame we sell. And the owner blamed me. Can you believe it?"

When I got home from school, I'd find her with her feet in a pot of hot water.

"That old lady is unbearable."

"What old lady?"

"The owner."

Heels cast off, and mamá ranting.

"Bad day again?"

"The worst!"

She was always in a bad mood now and it was best just to leave her, not ask questions.

I'd have lunch and she would change. I'd do my homework and she'd take a bath. I'd watch *Sesame Street* and she'd bring the clothes she'd worn that day down for Lucila to wash.

"By hand, do you hear me? I don't want this blouse getting damaged, Lucila, it's very delicate."

At night, over dinner, she complained about the owner, the customers, the exorbitant prices, the things she didn't sell, her wages.

It was a relief when she quit.

"The old bag was furious."

"What did she say?"

"She started taking a tone, scolding, and I finally gave her a piece of my mind."

"What did you say?"

"Everything right down to what she was going to die of."

When I got back from school, I'd find her in bed with a magazine. I'd eat lunch and she would turn pages. I'd do homework and she would turn pages. I'd watch *Sesame Street* and she would turn pages.

"Mamá," I said one Monday, "I need your help with some social-studies homework. You have to trace a map of Colombia and glue it into my notebook."

"Can't you do it yourself?"

"I can, but the teacher told us to ask our mothers."

She looked up from her magazine, checking to see if it was really true.

"I swear. She said it a thousand times."

"That your mothers should do your homework?"

"Yes. Trace the map from the atlas and glue it into our notebooks very carefully, so it's straight and vertical and all fits on one page, instead of horizontal on two. We're going to work on it all week."

"I don't understand."

"Come into the study and I'll show you."

I had everything all ready, laid out for her on the desk: the tracing paper, a pencil, the open atlas, my notebook, and the glue.

"You have to trace this map and stick it right here."

I pointed at the right-hand page of my notebook, up and down.

"Not like this."

I indicated both pages, left and right.

"It's very important for the whole thing to go on one page."

I showed her once more.

"Okay."

"Do you understand?"

"I said yes, Claudia."

She began tracing; I watched her hand. Which was boring, so I turned on the TV. *Sesame Street* was on, and it had started to seem like a dumb show. *Around-around-around-around, over, under, and through.* Please, that was kindergartner stuff. Still, when Ernie and Bert came out in their pajamas, one snoring and the other watching him, I was transfixed.

"All done," my mother said.

I half-turned.

"Thanks."

And immediately I turned back to the TV.

"Should I put your notebook in your schoolbag?"

"Okay."

Count von Count, in his castle full of bats, was still my favorite. *I count slowly, slowly, slowly getting faster, Once I start in counting it's very hard to stop, Faster, fast it is so exciting, I could count forever, count until I drop …*

I didn't open my notebook until the following day, when our social-studies teacher told us to. I couldn't believe it. The map was traced well, but glued in horizontally, over two pages. Exactly the opposite of what we'd been told. Exactly what the teacher had warned us not to do.

Thin, elderly, wearing a skirt down to her knees, her parted hair falling like two curtains, the teacher called us up to her desk in alphabetical order, one by one, to check our homework. She was giving each girl a check, you could tell.

My turn came. I got up, walked to her desk, and

handed her my notebook. I closed my eyes to take a breath. When I opened them, she had my notebook open and was holding it up to the class.

"Exactly the opposite of what you were told," she said in her penetrating voice that seemed like it was coming out of a sound system. "Exactly what I warned you not to do."

She lowered the notebook and stared at me.

"How do you explain this, señorita?"

I didn't say anything.

"You did not follow my instructions. Who would glue in a map like that? Look at this, it's awful." She closed my notebook disdainfully. "You did not ask your mother for help."

I looked up at her in surprise.

"Am I right?"

She had very dark brown eyes and the whites were all yellow. I looked at the class. All of the girls sat at their desks, awaiting an answer.

"Yes," I said, since I'd rather them think that I was the dummy who'd done a terrible job.

The teacher shook her head and handed back my notebook.

"You've earned a zero."

I watched her write it in the gradebook with a red pen and returned to my seat.

At recess, me and María del Carmen sat face to face with our lunchboxes.

"How are you going to make up that zero?"

The schoolyard was a cement slab with no grass or plants. Just a ton of girls, all the same in their uniforms, blue skirts and white shirts, knee socks, black shoes, all sitting like us or standing, talking, playing, running.

"I don't know."

"Why didn't you ask your mother for help?"

I was going to tell her the truth. That I had, I'd explained in detail exactly what my mother had to do and she still did it wrong, for no reason, because she didn't care about anything, not even me or my homework, just her magazines and her bed, and that she spent all day lying there doing nothing. I was about to start sobbing. I could feel the sob making its way up my throat like a hairball. But María del Carmen wasn't really asking, she was scolding. She kept talking:

"My mother says your mother is the prettiest, most elegant mother in our class."

The sob, the thick dry ball in my throat, got stuck halfway and I had to swallow it down.

"Seriously?"

"A perfect lady."

I tried to smile but what came out was my father's orphan expression. I don't know how María del Carmen couldn't tell, but she smiled at me, back to normal.

Lucila took my lunchbox.

"Miss Claudia."

We started walking.

"I hate my mother."

"Don't say that."

"She did my homework all wrong. The teacher showed it to the whole class and gave me a zero."

Lucila didn't say anything.

"I'm going to cut her hair off with scissors."

"Whose?"

"My mother's."

"Don't say that."

"I'm going to push her down the stairs."

"Even thinking that is a sin."

"And then I'm going to tell her the truth, that she's the worst mother in the world."

"Your poor mother; she's feeling very fragile right now."

"She is?"

"I had to water the plants today ..."

I looked at her. She kept her gaze straight ahead and neither of us said anything else.

Lucila opened the front door. It felt like the apartment was stiller than ever, the plants motionless, the space overtaken by silence. She went into the kitchen. With my schoolbag on my back, I climbed the stairs expecting nothing good, especially after what I'd said.

There was no light on in my parents' room. I took a couple of steps and peeked in. It was like a cave in there. Mamá was curled up in bed, breathing slowly, with the sheet over her even though it was hot. She looked so small, an old lady breathing her last, as though she'd wasted away while I was at school and this slow breathing was all that remained of her life.

She hadn't had any whisky since Rebeca's wake. Or allergy medicine. She wasn't walking around with a red nose, stuffed-up voice, box of Kleenex. I turned to the hall to look out the giant window, to see what state the guayacanes were in. They weren't in bloom.

Or bare. They'd recovered and had new buds on each branch.

The bare staircase, at my feet, with its slabs and black steel tubes, looked steeper than the cliff in the mountains, a vaster and more terrible abyss. The jungle below was thriving, its plants green and healthy. The afternoon wind blew in through the windows, the jungle awoke from its slumber and in the apartment, despite my mother, there was a celebration.

LISA DILLMAN lives in Atlanta, Georgia, USA, where she translates Spanish, Catalan, and Latin American writers and teaches in the department of Spanish and Portuguese at Emory University. Some of her recent translations include *A Silent Fury* by Yuri Herrera, *A Luminous Republic* by Andrés Barba, *The Touch System* by Alejandra Costamagna, and *The Bitch* by Pilar Quintana (shortlisted for the National Book Award in Translated Literature).

Book Club Discussion Guides on our website.

On the Design

As book design is an integral part of the reading experience, we would like to acknowledge the work of those who shaped the form in which the story is housed.

Tessa van der Waals (Netherlands) is responsible for the cover design, cover typography, and art direction of all World Editions books. She works in the internationally renowned tradition of Dutch Design. Her bright and powerful visual aesthetic maintains a harmony between image and typography, and captures the unique atmosphere of each book. She works closely with internationally celebrated photographers, artists, and letter designers. Her work has frequently been awarded prizes for Best Dutch Book Design.

The title is in Garage Gothic, a font that explores the coarse, unvarnished shapes of vernacular typography. Designer Tobias Frere-Jones based it on discarded parking tickets. The huge capital A of the title—in the same purple used on the cover of Quintana's *The Bitch*, also published by World Editions—evokes a precipice next to the abyss of the pitch-black backdrop. Inspired by Matisse, internationally renowned Dutch illustrator Annemarie van Haeringen made the floral jungle foliage by cutting and tearing colored papers, the visible white edges of which suggest depth. The author's name is in the Didonesque font by Paolo Goode.

The cover has been edited by lithographer Bert van der Horst of BFC Graphics (Netherlands).

Euan Monaghan (United Kingdom) is responsible for the typography and careful interior book design.

The text on the inside covers and the press quotes are set in Circular, designed by Laurenz Brunner (Switzerland) and published by Swiss type foundry Lineto.

All World Editions books are set in the typeface Dolly, specifically designed for book typography. Dolly creates a warm page image perfect for an enjoyable reading experience. This typeface is designed by Underware, a European collective formed by Bas Jacobs (Netherlands), Akiem Helmling (Germany), and Sami Kortemäki (Finland). Underware are also the creators of the World Editions logo, which meets the design requirement that "a strong shape can always be drawn with a toe in the sand."